We hope you enjoy this book. Please return or renew it by the due date.

You can renew it at www.norfolk.gov.uk/libraries or by using our free library app.

Otherwise you can phone 0344 800 8020 - please have your library card and PIN ready.

You can sign up for email reminders too.

NORFOLK COUNTY COUNCIL
LIBRARY AND INFORMATION SERVICE

GIBSON SQUARE

y Gibson Square in 2018

U
U

be identified as the author of this work has been asserted in accor-
Patents Act 1988.

natural, recyclable products made from wood grown in
vegetable based. Manufacturing conforms to ISO 14001,
C chain of custody schemes. Colour-printing is through a
that offsets its $CO_2$ emissions.

ation may be reproduced, stored in a retrieval system, or trans-
onic, mechanical, photocopying, recording or otherwise without
alogue record for this book is available from the Library of
t © Geoffrey Beattie.

For Laura

*'Gesture is the only speech and general language of the human nature… It speaks all languages, and as a universal character of reason, is generally understood and known by all nations.'*

*John Bulwer Chirologia: Or the Natural Language of the Hand and Chironomia: Or the Art of Manual Rhetoric, 1644*

# ONE

We were sitting in a darkened smoke-filled room, towards the far wall, where the smoke hung low like thick cloud. We had picked our seats carefully, not to be near the fog of smoke, but for other reasons.

He was already there in front of us. The hard nut who was going to do him. Mr. Big, we were calling him already, and we hadn't really seen him close up yet. Big Lenny had suggested the name. He knew a few Mr. Bigs. This was just another one. We were waiting for the others to arrive at the drinking club. We knew that there was going to be serious violence that night. We had heard all about Mr. Big, this Mr. Big, and what he was capable of.

'Serious violence'. I laugh when I catch myself saying it. It kind of slips off the tongue like other expressions worn down into cliché and euphemism. It slips between your fingers like a pellet of wet soap, hard to get hold of, slippery, evasive. It sounds like police argot. Loitering with intent, affray, and serious violence. Important sounding words, a bit slippery, that make something out of nothing to help the police out in their bureaucratic travails. Lenny liked using the expression. It became worn and smooth in his large horny hands. He threatened punters with it. The ordinary punters. 'Slippery fuckers,' he called them, 'all of them.'

So what did we really know about what was going to happen

that night in the club? We knew that somebody was going to lose their life that night. We knew that, and that's about as serious as you can get, even by Lenny's standards.

I checked the time by glancing at my watch. I wasn't as surreptitious as all that. I moved my arm up steadily against my body and pulled the sleeve of my jacket back slowly and carefully. But I could see the muscles of his eyes almost clench. 'Patience', whispered Big Lenny, out of the corner of his mouth. His bottom lip all extended. 'Patience. Just try and relax. You're making me nervous.' He stressed the nerve syllable of 'nervous' rather than the 'me'. I noticed that. I like to think that I'm a good observer of people.

He started to light up another cigarette. The match lisped twice across the sandpaper and then crackled into life. It sounded loud and intrusive in that room with all the tension hanging. This action of his made me anxious, but I didn't comment on it. The privileges of power, I thought to myself, privileges that he negotiated for himself through that mouth of his, and those large horny hands with knuckles that were misshapen and swollen. 'I've got knuckles on my knuckles,' he would say and the lads would all laugh. 'It takes years of careful nurturing to get them to look like this.'

I was somehow accountable for everything that I did in that room, but he wasn't. It seemed unfair, but that was the way he had made it. We sat side by side. We knew roughly what was going to happen that night in the drinking club. We had been warned. Or rather I had been warned. Lenny was my guest. I needed the support, he wanted to be in on it. 'I'm game for anything,' he said. 'Anything like this, that is.' And he had laughed, which I thought was curious. In anyone else I would interpret it as a sign of tension, but not in him.

I was just waiting quietly for what I knew was inevitable, not the murder itself but a wave of revulsion to hit me. It wasn't the victim I was concerned about. It was me. I had to watch it all, in front of Lenny. Like a child on a sea shore in a storm watching the tides roll towards me. A violence that could not be stopped, or turned back at this stage. There was an inevitability about the whole thing. I glanced at Big Lenny. His bulk reassured me. I was new to this game; I was the child here. I watched the calluses on his hand move towards his mouth, and the ash of the cigarette glow in the half light, like a red pulsating ganglion. The thought occurred to me that this is all we are. A collection of pulsating nerves that could be extinguished by a guy like him over there, the guy sitting with the beer in his hand at the bar. Not a care in the world. Or a guy like Lenny. Carefree individuals, careless with other people's lives.

I had once asked Lenny if he had ever killed anybody. It was the sort of question that I thought might break the ice one cold night outside his club when he had stopped me from going in. He liked to stop me sometimes just for the nobble. Just for the nobble, that's what he always said. Just in case I was taking too much for granted. So I had to hang about outside with him and the rest of the bouncers, stomping up and down in their over-coats, keeping themselves warm, keeping themselves amused at my expense. They were all laughing at me. Men with big stiff necks that hardly moved. They had to swing their shoulders to turn my way to view my discomfort.

He moved me to one side with a sweeping movement of his large hand to let the other punters in, the blistered palm towards me and upright, in a slow semi-circular motion. 'Good evening, sir. Good evening, madam,' he said to a couple arriving at the door with gold clanking on their unnatural winter tans and a curious synchronicity in their appearance with matching blond streaks in their hair tumbling down over similar styled jackets.

Big Lenny, the official greeter of the great movers and shakers in Sheffield — 'Steel City', they called it. 'Nice to see you again, young sir,' he said to a man with biggish hair and a tight, over-used grimace for a smile, who glanced at me and pretended to shiver. I stood in the cold up against the wall, attracting superior, haughty looks from those who were allowed to enter the club without having to endure the indignity of the knock-back. The bouncers periodically rotated towards me and laughed. They had all the power here.

So I asked my question about killing. And why not? I assumed that it was the kind of thing that Lenny and his friends talked about out there in the cold with all that social intercourse going on behind those gold-flecked doors, in the perfumed warmth of the club. 'What?' Lenny said, the quick delivery sounded like a bird squawking. There was no 't' sound. It came out like 'whaaaa-.' He came slowly over to me with this bewildered expression out in front of him. 'Whaaaa-?' He squawked again, in my face. He was so close that I could smell his minty breath. He was always very particular about this. He sucked on Polo mints more or less continuously when he was working the door. He would some-times have two or three in his mouth at the same time. You could hear them rattle against his teeth when he was preparing to talk. I was waiting for them to stop.

'I'm a professional,' he said. 'I've been dealing with punters for years. I served my apprenticeship dealing with drunks, guys as high as a kite, druggies, coke heads and speed freaks. I've had to eject lefties, righties, rejects from Khomeini's Iran up in Steel City because they got chucked out after the revolution, Arabs, Eyeties, Frogs. Once a whole team of frog footballers in their official jackets. I've had to fight Paddies, Pakis and Chinks. I always judge it right. No unnecessary force is my motto. Do you understand me?'

I said that I did, but I had watched him knock drunk punters spark out, his words not mine, spark out down concrete steps. Paddies, Pakis and Chinks, spark out in puddles of their own making. Deep red and black puddles streaked with vomit and piss. I had watched ambulances take them away across town, with Big Lenny and his friends waving good-bye. Big Lenny was rarely even picked up for anything by the police. He got on well with the local police, and the CID. They seemed almost to admire each other in an odd and unhealthy kind of way. 'I nearly joined the police,' he would say. 'You're better off out of it,' Cliff, the police inspector, would say. 'It's all hands behind your back stuff. It's shit really.'

So Lenny had nearly joined the police, or so he said, but had he ever killed anybody? I still didn't know. But he was looking forward to the action that night in that smoky room we were watching, with me trying to keep myself calm and composed. Ready for anything. I was taking my lead from him. Every time he put the cigarette to his mouth, I felt my finger move towards my mouth, and I nibbled my nail in a sort of synchronous movement with his smoking. I wasn't biting my nails, I never have. Nibbling is really the wrong word for it. There were no ragged edges. My nail just wiped across my lips which closed in on it. There was a lot of hand to mouth contact. It was better than sucking my thumb.

My copying of the timing of his movements made him edgy. It's not supposed to do this from all the science that I'd ever read. But it was as if he could sense a shadow following him in the dark. I could see it in his face. A momentary stillness crossing it, as if he was waiting to see what would happen to the shadow, when all of his tics and tremors and smaller more significant movements were dampened down. Like Lenny's well muscled boxer dog on the street when it has seen that piece of white furry, feline flesh flagrantly wandering along so carefree and so provocatively past him. The hard muscle body, moving perpetually with all the breathing in and breathing out, suddenly becoming quite still. Listening, waiting, fixed on its target, all senses attenuated and strained. Quite still, ready for that cat.

I had seen the dog many times. He often brought it with him when he visited me. He called it Butch, but he pronounced it 'Bootch'. It was just one of his little jokes. It sounded effeminate.

'Bootch, come here,' he would shout on the street, extending the 'oo' sound, just to watch the faces of the passers-by. It was a little dig at nobody in particular in that street. A little warning salvo. Just a nobble is what he called it.

I thought that his dog had very poor eye sight. Poor eye sight and very short legs for something that was meant to be a pedigree boxer. But you couldn't mention either of these things. He was proud of that animal. Butch seemed to think that anything white was a cat and therefore a potential victim. It could hardly discriminate. Litter, a plastic canister, and last winter a snowman with a carrot for a nose were all cats as far as Bootch was concerned. Anything white and the dog would stand quite still and its breathing would start to diminish. Watching for signs of movement from the snowman that never budged, or the scrap of newspaper that might be lifted up by the wind and thrown across the street, causing Bootch endless excitement in the process as he tracked his victim's every movement.

I stopped biting my nails, and I could see Lenny's body go back to life again. I was nervous, I admit that. I could feel my nerves jangling away inside me, the adrenaline careering through my body in arcs towards my extremities which felt a little numb. My mouth was dry, almost salty to the taste. I could feel myself flicking the roof of my mouth with my tongue. This action was making a soft clicking sound, like a dog gently lapping water from a bowl. Lenny told me to be quiet.

I was trying to stop myself displaying my nervousness in front of him. I sat with my fingers interlocked to stop them trembling, to stop them leaking any nervous energy. My fingers rubbed on the bones of my thin smooth knuckles, and then tried to find sanctuary in the crevasses at the base of my fingers. I crossed my ankles so that at least one of my feet would be off the ground and therefore not be tap, tap, tapping on the floor with an irritating, incessant, dead give-away beat. I kept staring straight ahead at the door, so that Lenny would only ever get a side view of my face.

That would be less revealing I thought. I wouldn't leak anxiety or fear from the side of my face quite so easily.

I tried to keep my jaw relaxed. I tried to let it hang open, gaping and wide. I had thought about keeping it taut so that when the violence did come, there would be no change in my facial expression. But I didn't want any comments as to why I was just sitting there beside him, grimacing away. He might think that I had indigestion, or something worthy of comment. I couldn't bear him making some kind of crack about it. I was too tense to laugh or smile or make any jibe back, the way that you must do if somebody plays that sort of game. I had been around Lenny long enough to know that this is how you must respond if somebody makes a crack. Never let an insult stand, that's what he always said. Always give as good as you get. If you don't you're a nobody.

I had learnt this the hard way. Big Lenny had seen some punter one night saying something to me in his club. I had brushed against the guy's arm and spilled a little of his drink. The club was packed. I just swayed his way with the crowd and knocked into him, and some lager was spilled out of his full glass as he bent forward for a sip. It was no big deal. Nothing to get excited about.

'Fucking clumsy wanker,' said the guy with wet running down his chin. He said it quietly, almost below his breath. 'Sorry,' I replied. 'Sorry about that.' And then I tried to walk away. Lenny, standing by the pillar with mirrors on each side, watched me walk a pace or two and then caught me by the arm. He pulled me in close to his chest so that I could smell his sweat and his after-shave, which he sprayed himself with for free in the gents' toilet. 'Ten pence a shot', the sign in there warned. 'Pay up'. But this rule didn't apply to Big Lenny, few rules ever did.

'I think that I must be fucking hearing things,' he whispered in my ear. 'I must have spent too many nights in noisy night clubs. My hearing must have gone. Or perhaps it was all those years in the steel mills. That must be it. That must be why my hearing is completely fucked. What did he just say to you?'

'It was nothing,' I said. 'Nothing.' I tried to sound casual, care-free.

'Oh, alright then,' said Lenny, and then he pulled me closer until I was nestling on his chest. 'What did he say to you?'

Lenny held me just by the elbow and squeezed harder on the nerve, literally squeezing the truth out of me, like juice from an orange. He always liked to say to his CID pals that if they had the same freedom as he had they would get the truth out of the bad guys a lot quicker. They always talked about the bad guys. I always wondered who these bad guys were, as the CID wandered around the club on duty, drinking their complimentary pints, talking to Lenny and the lads on the door about the bad guys. The guys in dark corners, the guys who worked rival doors perhaps. The bad guys.

'He said something like "fucking clumsy", I think,' I replied.

'No, he did not,' said Lenny. 'He did not say that. He said "fucking clumsy *wanker*".' And just in case I didn't get it, he made a movement with his forefinger and thumb, like a bottle being shaken. 'He has just called you a fucking tosspot and you're going to leave it at that?' Lenny said. 'You're pathetic. Do you know that?' Lenny took a large step back towards the man still slowly and deliberately drying his chin with his girlfriend's paper hand-kerchief. Lenny had a motionless smirk on his face.

'Hey,' he said. 'You've just wet our carpet. I thought that you'd pissed yourself for a minute. Perhaps you could try to hold it in until you get home next time.'

I watched the reflection of the man's face in the mirror on the pillar. Lenny had shown me this trick. You can watch all the comings and goings that way without ever being noticed. Lenny spent a lot of time looking in tinted mirrors.

'Eh?' said the man with the spilt drink.

'You heard,' said Big Lenny.

'That guy knocked my arm,' said the man, pointing aggres-sively at me. 'Him with his back to us. That guy over there. The one who is deliberately ignoring us.'

'What did you say again?' said Lenny quickly, pointing at his ears, tapping them, as if he was indeed deaf from the small number of years he had spent in the steel mills and the large number of years he had spent in clubs like this.

'THAT FUCKER KNOCKED MY ARM,' repeated the man. 'THAT CUNT OVER THERE.'

'Right, that's enough of that abusive shouting in here. You're out.' Lenny grabbed him by the throat and pushed him back against the wall. 'Walk quietly,' he said.

'Oh fucking hell,' the girlfriend said. 'Don't batter him for fuck's sake. He's staying with me tonight. I don't want any blood on the pillow cases. My mother will kill me when she gets back from her boyfriend's.'

'Take it easy for fuck's sake,' said the guy whose chin was now dry through all that pushing and shoving and rubbing and heaving. 'I'm going to come quietly.'

As soon as he turned to walk Lenny got both arms around his neck in a smooth continuous movement and pulled him backwards until just his heels touched the carpet. Lenny walked backwards towards the nearest fire exit with the man gurgling away in front of him, like a helpless baby.

'Don't make him sick for fuck's sake,' said the girlfriend. 'He'll be up all night puking. He's used all my paper hankies up already drying himself.'

The DJ spotted the crowd parting to let this unlikely triumvirate through. Lenny and then the man, and then a few paces behind his girlfriend, who suddenly realized that their big night out was coming to an end. It was trouble alright.

'Door staff to lower cocktail bar, quick. Alpha priority. Door staff to lower bar. Alpha rating. Alpha! Get a move on lads.'

Big Norman and Wee Steve bustled through the crowd. Lenny was shouting instructions to his team. 'Get that fucking blonde bird,' he shouted to Steve. 'She's in on it as well.'

She had taken her white stiletto off and was trying to hit her boyfriend in the face with it. Lenny was strangling her boyfriend with one arm and trying to shield him with the other.

She was irate. 'You've ruined our fucking engagement celebration, you selfish cunt. You self-centred fucking twat. My mother was right. You're no fucking good.'

I watched Steve grab her from behind and move his hands up across her sides and then onto her ample chest, pinning her arms to the side. 'Come, on love,' he said, 'calm down.' He was saying this in an almost seductive way, as if he was trying to chat her up. His hands stayed where they were. Steve always said that this was one of the perks of the job, looking after the birds when their boyfriends were being shown the door. That's how he described it. Looking after them.

Her boyfriend was kicking and screaming now. His face white with anger, saliva all around his mouth. Big Norman thumped him on the nose. That's what they did when they wanted to make the punter really angry. It was the chin to pacify them, it was the nose to gee them up, especially when they were already restrained and when Steve was getting a feel. I heard the crack, and then after a long, long pause, the blood started pouring in a stop-go movement like clotted cream down his white shirt.

I walked away. I had to. I couldn't watch this anymore. The voice in my head told me to. I heard the door of the fire exit being kicked open and the blonde screaming. Not in anger, but in pain. Somebody must have popped her. Perhaps it was the boyfriend. I couldn't make out what she was saying. I pushed against the crowd who were all shuffling in the opposite direction to me, going towards the action for a better look. I watched their faces, unconsciously set in anticipation. Eyes widened to take in all of the spectacle in front of them. I stood quietly on my own in a small deserted patch in the middle of a busy night-club. The DJ winked down at me, and then leant down from the DJ console.

'It's going to be a good one tonight, I can feel it in my water,' he said. 'And now,' he said turning to the microphone, 'a very special song, the Hot Chocolate classic "It started with a kiss".'

Lenny came back in to find me. He stood beside me, his arms folded across his chest. He looked pleased with himself. Another little lesson. 'You caused all this,' he said. 'You know that, don't you? You set all this in motion because you don't know how to act. You can't let cunts like that insult you. Otherwise, they'll shit all over you. And then they would get carried away and start to think that they could shit all over other people as well. And then where would we all be?'

I shrugged my shoulders. He made a 'hmmmmph' noise and walked off, smug and satisfied. The enforcer, he liked to call himself sometimes, from the Clint Eastwood film. The enforcer of the rules of social etiquette and social division in this town in the North of England in the deepest and longest of recessions with the unemployed blowing their unemployment benefit on one night in his club pretending to be something that they were not.

He left me alone to ponder. You have to give as good as you get. I didn't know how. There were rules, I knew that. They were complex, intricate rules, like rules of grammar. These were rules of *interactional* grammar specifying what was permissible and what wasn't in any response to an insult. The rules constrained the topic, the structure and even the intonation pattern to be used in any response. That's how I thought about it. It must have been my academic training. I had worked this out for myself from the hundreds of examples that he presented me with. I had built up somewhere in my head a large corpus of his insults.

I just had to infer the rules from this corpus. Just. As if it was that easy. What did I know? I knew that you had to make negative comments about actual characteristics of the person without causing personal insult. Height, build, amount of bodily fat, sexual preference, shoe size, they were all fair game. But there was a lot more to it than that. How much more I wasn't quite sure.

Lenny always said that the point was to see how far you could go without causing real personal offence. Right up to the brink. He was good at it. I had watched him hundreds of times trading insults. As quick as a flash, the insult would be slapped back in the face of the punter with interest. No obvious pauses for reflection or planning, no perceptible delay in its production. Like tennis, but that's too middle class an analogy, back and forward, thwack, thwack, as smooth as you like. Until the other guy faltered. Until the other guy blinked. He could anticipate what was coming. That was his secret. It was uncanny sometimes to listen to. That degree of anticipation.

He seemed to have lots of these insults stored in his brain, ready to be modified slightly and then pulled out to be used. It was as if a major part of his social life consisted of these little semi-automatic routines for everyday use. It told me something about the automaticity of everyday life.

He enjoyed these confrontations. He liked taking people to the edge. And leaving them there. And when it all tumbled over the brink he liked that too Perhaps he liked that best of all. Perhaps, that was his secret. There was no real brink, as far as he was concerned. 'You do whatever is necessary,' he said. I always thought that he lived a complex and dangerous but ultimately a very orderly life.

I didn't want to get into any of this routine the night of the serious violence, so I decided against a taut grimacing face that would not be affected by any gore or any killing. I kept my jaw slightly apart, my mouth slightly open.

'That's a good lad,' said Lenny, 'hang loose.'

I wasn't accustomed to serious violence right in front of me. Right on my lap, so to speak. Big Lenny, on the other hand, had worked on doors for years. He was used to it. He always said that he had seen everything. He said that nothing could surprise him any longer. There was a weariness about how he said it sometimes, so that you just had to believe it. But the weariness was part of the act. I knew that he loved it all. He had been attacked with bottles, hammers, coshes, knuckle dusters, penknives, Stanley knives, machetes, screwdrivers, beer crates, shoes, stilettos, brief-cases, metal files, doors, chests of drawers, wardrobes, cars, vans, fans, fan heaters, electric fires. The list was unordered and virtu-ally endless. 'Try to name one object that I haven't been attacked with,' he would ask.

His one joke about the list was that the weapons used against him were once dangerous tools of work before Thatcher got going, and started closing down British Steel, and then started shutting the mines. She had taken the hammers, the Stanley knives and the screwdrivers off the violent punters. She had dis-armed them herself. She had done all that for law and order in Britain.

But they weren't disarmed. They were just using other things now. Now it was all instruments of leisure that they wanted to fight with, according to Lenny, pens, women's combs with the ends sharpened, bottles and camping knives rather than Stanley knives. That was what Thatcher had really done for law and order in this country, she had confiscated the work tools off the violent punters and given them sharpened combs to fight with instead.

Lenny said that the types of weapons men and women used in fights in and around Sheffield were a good index of the econom-ic climate in the North of England. Better than any of those made-up economic statistics from London anyway.

I was thinking about this joke of his. It helped me relax a little. My jaw had gone a bit wobblier for the first time. I could feel it move. I thought of some of his other jokes. He had told me one night in the club where he worked that he had been attacked with parts of an animal. He used this in a guessing game to pass the night away outside the clubs where he worked.

'What part of an animal was shoved in my kisser?' he would ask. The other doormen would all have to guess. All the doormen in Sheffield knew the correct answer. It was part of the knowledge, part of knowing the score around here.

I knew the answer, but it didn't make me one of the guys in the know. Clearly not. You needed other qualities as well. I was more of a hanger-on. Not one of the lads.

One night on a door in Chesterfield, Big Lenny had had a load of pigs' feet pushed in his face by a butcher's son during a fight. He told me that he had made sure that he got the address of the shop where the man worked off another doorman and he hand delivered the dry cleaning bill to the man responsible the next day.

'Big greasy stains,' he had told me, 'up and down my DJ. Big greasy stains. They were even on my bow tie. I went round there the next day in my suit and tie and I made sure that he paid up there and then. He asked me if I would take a cheque. The nerve of some people. "I only deal in cash", I said. "I am an integral part of the cash economy of this country. Go, fuck yourself." He had to go and nick the money out of his dad's till to pay me.'

'And what was this butcher's son doing with pigs' feet in a night-club?' you might well ask. That was my response to the story. None of the bouncers ever asked him. It's funny that. They just accepted the story as it was, but I always thought that it was the logical thing to enquire about. I mean what was somebody doing with pigs' feet in a nightclub? It's not that I didn't believe the story, it was just that I wanted to understand it better. It was the kind of response that might be expected from a hanger-on, a man who didn't know the score. 'Fuck knows?' is all Lenny ever said when I asked him. He would get annoyed when asked, as if I was querying it. I just couldn't help myself. I suppose that it was because of my education. 'I think that they were for his supper or something. I never asked him. It never came up in the conversation, fucking Muppet-head.'

'Muppet-head.' I should have said something back to him that very instant when he called me that. Something to do with Muppets. That was the over-arching topic, and then something personal about him. Something really insulting without causing offence. But what? 'Fuck off, you bald-headed Kermit.' 'You should have enquired, Miss Piggy.' Something like that. I ran several of these through my mind but nothing satisfactory came out in time. Thankfully. So I was a Muppet-head whenever I asked about the pigs' feet, and I let it stand.

Lenny always laughed when he told the story about the pigs' feet, when he wasn't asked, that is, about where the pigs' feet came from. The story, like Lenny himself, had done the rounds. Night after night in the frosty air outside different clubs in Sheffield, you would hear this and other stories. They got embellished through time, but not that much. Doormen liked the raw urgency of the genuine article, a story that was not too well-crafted nor contrived. They could tell the real thing, even if the logic was left just hanging there sometimes.

Our night waiting for the action to unfold in this drinking club would be a story one day, I thought to myself. I hoped it would make more sense than some of the others.

Lenny had been hardened by his years on doors, and become opinionated through them. These were my conclusions anyway based on what I knew about him. He said that he had always been like that. Always hard, since his father, over from Dublin, had been laid off work and took to the drink. 'We were the first wogs in this country, the first proper nig nogs, before they started picking on the blacks,' he said. 'My dad went to some digs and there was a sign outside this real shit house of a place saying "No dogs and no Irish." They painted "Irish bastards go home", on our backyard wall in bright green letters. They wouldn't dare write it on the front wall.'

Lenny often managed to find something positive in even the most depressing of situations. 'Cowards, you see. They wouldn't say it to your face or try to get the paint out at the front of your house.'

Door work, he always said, had just firmed him up a bit, and confirmed all his prejudices and stereotypes, of which there were many. The Paddies like a good fight when they've had a drink, but they don't bear grudges when they've sobered up, Pakis like to use knives, Southerners won't fight unless they've got plenty of back-up, women are just as bad as men in fights, and just as vicious and just as nasty. He treated all trouble makers the same way. An arm lock with his big mutton-deep forearms, then a sideways or back-wards drag along the floor, keeping them off balance at all times, their toes just skimming the surface of the dance floor, and then a gratuitous smack for their trouble. Finally, a push out onto the street for them to become somebody else's problem. 'Get shot of them,' he would say, 'as quickly as possible. Just get shot. I want a quiet life and these people are stopping me having it.'

But I had never seen him so nervous before. I started thinking that what was about to happen might be too 'tasty' even for him. 'Tasty', that's a word he liked applying to violence. When I had told him about what was going to happen in the club that night, he had offered himself up immediately. 'Nice and tasty,' he had said at the time. 'Just the way I like it.' And I swear I saw him lick his big fat, cracked lips as he said it. I can't explain that action. I thought that it might be a conscious act, a deliberate attempt to show me how hard he really was. So I asked him to repeat the action, right there in front of me. Casual like, the way he might do it.

My logic was impeccable. If it was at all conscious, or if it was all just a deliberate act, then he should be able to repeat it on request. If somebody gives you the V-sign, for example, the fingers, then they know what they're doing. It's a conscious mean-ingful act, we know exactly what it means, and therefore it's repeatable. On the other hand, if somebody just gestures as they talk, and the gestures are just those apparently vague movements that go along with everyday speaking then you can't repeat them. They're sub-conscious, and you might not even know that you've been moving at all. You've just got a vague sense of something going on, but not much, nothing definite.

That was my logic. I didn't explain the logic to him, I'm not that daft. I just made my request as casually as possible.

'Repeat what you've just done,' I said to Lenny, as he finished licking his lips and smiling that night in the wine bar earlier.

'Repeat what?' said Lenny with this look on his face. It was a blend of an expression really, half incredulity, half sneer. It was a common expression for that big face of his. 'What you've just done with your facial apparatus,' I replied. 'What?' he said. 'What facial apparatus?'

'Look, just try to do what you've just done,' I said. 'For me. Go on, just try. Just repeat what you've just done and say the words too. That might help you.'

So he made a stupid face, part innocence, part surprise this time and said, 'Nice (pause) and (pause) tasty,' pausing after each word to watch my response. He had remembered what he had said alright, but there was no tongue movement. None at all.

So it wasn't conscious after all, I thought. He really does lick his lips like that, when it comes to considerations of violence. There are some things that are very hard to understand in people. Even for me.

Or he had seen through my test. This on reflection was probably the most likely explanation.

# TWO

I watched Lenny slowly pull on his cigarette, the cigarette nestling in the cup of his hand. He was concentrating hard on the action in front of us. The man in the leather jacket with his girlfriend were sitting to the right of the bar away from the door. We were watching them at an angle, but we could see most of his face and a good slice of hers too. His girlfriend was blonde, her blonde curls bobbed around a bit whenever she spoke. She was wearing a black leather dress. You could see that she was sexy even from that angle, protruding out of the dress. She was the kind of girl who might elicit comments from any strange man that she might pass in a club. The kind of girl who provoked trouble, Lenny would say.

He had her placed immediately in a number of logically inter-connected categories. Tease, trouble-starter, potential headache. You could see it in his face, all that categorization immediately obvious in how he looked at her. His own girlfriend wasn't attrac-tive. He said that he preferred it like that.

He needed to provide a quiet commentary on the characters in front of us. He often did. He always talked about people behind their backs, and to their faces as well to be honest. He talked about them in the third person right in front of them. 'Look at this loser here,' he would say. 'No brains, or he wouldn't be stand-ing in my face provoking me like that.' And then sometimes the hand would shoot out. 'Wham, bam thank you ma'am. Don't say you weren't warned,' he would say, but they weren't warned, they were discussed, but never warned.

Lenny took a drag of his ciggie. 'She's the kind of bird,' he started, 'that is always responsible, always responsible for guys kicking off in clubs.' He turned his head slightly towards me to check my response. 'Always.' I nodded back quickly and surreptiously.

'If you banned birds like that from clubs, my job would be a lot fucking easier,' he whispered.

'Yeah', I replied. I said it so quietly that it sounded as if I was just breathing out. 'A lot fucking easier,' he repeated.

'You know this,' he said leaning towards me, looking eager, emphasizing the 'know'. 'In fact, you've probably got a fucking theory for it. Guys only fight when they've got something to fight over. Something like that down there. It's the fucking caveman in us, isn't that right? Some bollocks like that. We want her in the cave on her back and the dinosaur meat on the fucking table for afters.'

'Yeah,' I said. 'It's something like that. Now shoooosh.' And I felt my hot damp breath on his face. The man in the leather jacket and the girl in the sexy dress were talking intimately. They were leaning towards each other, both leaning about equally. I think that can be important. Equality of lean, that is. It seems to me to be more significant than the lean itself. He was looking at her straight in the eyes. I could see that without knowing exactly where she was looking. His eyes had a fixed focus, they weren't all over the place, which can be significant too. His hand was on top of hers on the bar. We couldn't hear any words, but we could see that he was doing most of the talking. I looked around the bar area. Lenny's eyes followed mine. There was a painting of Winston Churchill on one wall with a cigar in one hand. Lenny noticed it as well.

'What's this place called by the way?' asked Lenny quietly,

wishing to display his vigilance. 'It's not Churchill's by any chance, is it? Or Winston's?'

I said that I wasn't sure. Sometimes you miss details like this. It was just a smoky drinking den, that's all I knew, and we were sitting watching all the action within it.

The conversation we were focusing on was becoming quite animated. The man was gesturing a lot. I don't think that he was annoyed at her, he was just involved in what he was saying. Lenny nudged me. 'He's getting keyed up about something. Look at his hands,' said Lenny. I did. I would have noticed them anyway. There were a series of short stabbing beats in the space in front of his chest, just to the right of the midline. They were emphasizing the words, coinciding with the stress points of the sentence. They were quite violent. But that's a very loaded word. Quite brisk, stabbing movements, I mean. Brisk, batonic movements, that's about as neutral as I can get, although that sounds a little artistic. Like a conductor's baton. The movements were neither violent nor artistic. Just brisk.

'He's an aggressive sort of guy,' said Lenny. 'Look at the way he's talking to her. You need to keep an eye on aggressive guys like that in clubs. Guys who are always stabbing the air with their fingers.'

But then the short, sharp stabbing movements stopped and his hand rested peacefully again on hers. 'What is he now?' I asked. 'Has he changed his personality?'

'He's just taking a breather,' Lenny whispered. 'He's still an aggressive cunt, but he's just worn himself out, that's all.'

She leant forward and kissed him. I looked away. I couldn't help it. It felt intrusive to watch. I felt embarrassed. Lenny just kept staring, taking it all in.

'Well, what I always say is that this is a lot better than fighting,' he whispered. 'Better for them and better for us, better for all of us. And better to watch,' he added.

I glanced back. The man in the leather jacket was ordering

some more drinks from the barman, an elderly man with grey hair and false teeth that didn't seem to fit properly. You could see that whenever he tried to smile. We were close enough to them to be able to make out this level of detail.

'How many drinks has your man had?' asked Lenny. 'I hope that you're keeping count. You're the clever one. You keep the tally. That might be important.'

It was then that the door opened and in he came with two friends. 'Oh, oh,' said Lenny. 'We're on. Is that him? Is that your man?'

I looked through the smoky haze. It was hard to make anything out over by the door, the light was bad over there, but I thought that it must be him. It was about time that he arrived. I had never seen him before. 'Yes,' I said, 'I think that's him.'

'He's a big lad,' said Lenny, looking at his height and his shape in the doorway. 'A right big lad. They both are. This is going to be very tasty.'

I looked out for the tongue lick, but none came. I noticed that my lips had gone very dry. My hands clasped each other tightly across my abdomen; I could feel myself oozing perspiration. I rubbed my palms against each other in a vain attempt to dry them. The room felt even hotter. The adrenaline was making me feel a little queasy. The three men sat down at the bar a few feet from the couple. I noticed that the girl in the sexy dress looked round at them almost immediately. We had a better view of her face. She was very pretty. 'She's very tasty as well,' said Lenny. 'Did she smile at any of them?'

'I don't think so,' I said.

'But they've noticed her and they know her,' said Lenny. 'You can see that in their faces and their little sly looks at each other. They knew that she was going to be here. They've found her, their looks tell you that. And look at the guy in the leather jacket's face.'

We could see him clearly. His expression had changed. I admit that. It changed quickly, and the new expression that had taken over his face stayed there without any perceptible movement. We both noticed the change even from that distance.

Lenny exhaled some air in a long, blowing movement. 'Phooooooooow. He means business. That look says, "Don't fucking mess with me or my bird." I think that those three guys are too pissed to notice. That's the problem with drink. That's why people get into so much trouble when they're pissed up.'

'Do you think that he's consciously saying that with his expression? Or do you think that it's subtler than that?' I whispered.

'How should I know?' replied Lenny. 'I'm just telling you what I see. I'm an expert on that, and I can tell you that his look is saying ...'

'Signalling? Do you mean?' I said, interrupting him. 'Do you mean *signalling*?'

Lenny turned to look at me. He was scowling.

'Alright *signalling* then. He's signalling that he wants these three fuckers to fuck off and leave him and his girlfriend alone,' whispered Lenny. 'You see my reading of it is that the one in the grey suit, the one nearest her, did the tasty bird perhaps when the guy in the leather jacket was away on business or something. The guy in the grey suit knows her intimately. You can see that from his body language. He's not really facing the bar, he's facing her, and look at how wide apart his legs are. He's saying "come and climb aboard." She doesn't want to give the game away, that's why she won't even say "hello" to him.'

I noticed that the two men in dark suits were in exactly the same posture as each other - arms folded, legs tucked under the counter of the bar, head slightly rotated. But the other one, the man in the grey suit was in quite a different posture to them. He was orientated exclusively towards the blonde in the sexy dress, who was clearly with somebody else.

'Just wait for the sparks to fly,' said Lenny in a hushed tone. 'Just wait. It's pretty obvious what's going on down there. The guy in the grey suit has done her. That's why he and his pals have come tonight. He wants a bit more of what he got the last time. Your man in the leather jacket doesn't know about this, but he suspects. That's probably what they were talking about earlier. That's why he was getting so hot under the collar. He was going to give her the third degree and then your man walks in with his pals. Well, that tells him all that he needs to know, doesn't it? And his face tells me all that I need to know. Just look at that face now. He could murder the three of them.'

I looked at the facial expression of the man in the leather jacket and I had never seen an expression like it. Not in books, not in film depictions of violence, not on the street, not in any clubs that I had been to. It was a prolonged stare over his girlfriend's shoulder at the man in the grey suit. It was the immobility of the expression that was so new and so dangerous and beyond the myth of film, which prefers faster, more fleeting images that are meant to say it all. She could see it as well, directed out past her, not changing or flickering or altering or transmogrifying into something else. She reached out her hand to stop him moving, which seemed like an almost contradictory action given that there was so little movement coming from him. It was a look that meant business. The imminent action of this dangerous man seemed to be signaled through the very immobility of his expression.

I thought of Butch for a second. It was just a mental image of Butch from the back tracking the scrap of paper tossed in the air by the wind. It was Butch's pose before he struck. Quite still before he pounced.

The man in the grey suit smiled back at the man with the immobile face, a wavering sideways smile, almost a real smile of enjoyment with the muscles around the eyes working overtime, as if he was really enjoying the whole thing. Enjoying the situation.

'He's pissed for a start,' said Lenny. 'He must be. Get yourself ready. It's going to kick off in a second.'

It was an odd exchange between two men who did not seem

to know each other. One had hate written all over his face in this long, uninterrupted stare, and one looked as if he hadn't a care in the world. They looked at each other for perhaps a full minute. No words were exchanged. It was all done through that set of looks. A whole world of meaning somehow contained within them. It was like children in a staring game without the effort. That was what was so odd about it, it all looked so effortless. There were few blinks that we could see.

Then I noticed that the man in the leather jacket seemed to be trembling. That was at least my perception of the whole thing. 'He's trembling,' I said in a whisper. 'He's shaking with anger more like,' said Lenny. 'Trembling my arse. That's a shake not a tremble. A tremble is gentler than that. He's going to blow in a few seconds.'

We sat there in the darkened room waiting. I sneaked a last glance at Lenny's face. I had never seen him concentrating so hard. He didn't notice that I was looking. That was unusual for him.

Then something started to happen. Not suddenly, but slowly and deliberately. The man in the grey suit said something to the man in the leather jacket. We couldn't hear what he was saying. He made a small gesture. His right hand was out-stretched, then it started to make a claw, then a fist. The fore-finger and middle finger together dragging the others behind. He seemed to stop talking. Then he reached his hand out again. Lenny nudged me.

The hand settled on the back of the girl in the leather dress and moved slowly in a gentle smooth arc down the back of her shiny leather dress onto the top right hand side of her backside. You could see the disbelief on the man in the leather jacket's face. Just plain disbelief turning to horror. He had seen the hand moving towards her and had to guess where it had now settled. I had never seen a face like that before. Horror which turned in slow time into murderous rage. I almost have to invent the categories as I go along. Murderous rage. That's about as extreme as I can get.

His hand went up inside his coat. 'We're on,' said Lenny. 'This is it. This is what we're here for.'

I saw the blade. It didn't flash in such a darkened room. I recognized it from its outline, its fragile shape. He pulled it out of his coat, not a Stanley knife. Something longer and wider. Lenny would recognize it, I thought, he could give it a name. The other man's hands pulled back away from the girl in the dress. He must have been drunk. The action was too slow to help him. His stool tilted backwards as he retracted his hands. He fell back onto the floor. The man in the leather jacket stumbled on top of him. There was no pause. He stuck the knife in. It went easily through his jacket. The other two men bolted for the door and ran out onto the street. The door banging against its frame let some raw light into that corner, and you could see the knife splashing the air with streaks of light and blood. The wide blade going in, not once but three times, in a fluent movement with what seemed like hardly any resistance.

You could see the blood, spurting in a thin jet, marking the temporal boundaries of the stabbing movement, like commas between clauses. I suppose that because of my education I sometimes think in terms of text and the printed page. Lenny wouldn't have seen it like that.

The girl in the leather dress was mouthing a scream, but it was quite silent as far as we were concerned, as if the horror of it all had taken all her breath away. The barman with the false teeth had somehow disappeared. Lenny later claimed that he was so perceptive that he saw the man's teeth fall out as he ran. We couldn't see where he was at that moment in time. Lenny just said that he had got offside quick without his teeth.

Lenny and I were rooted to the spot. The man in the leather jacket took his time, he got up slowly and dusted himself down, although why he dusted down a leather jacket covered in blood I will never know. It was just a little act that seemed to say that everything was cool, everything was okay. There was no dust, and you can't remove blood with a slight wave of your hand. It was not a functional act. Signalling, that's the word for it. He was signalling that everything was cool. Then he led the girl out. The girl who was the cause of all the carnage, according to Big Lenny.

I noticed the time. I don't know why I looked. I just did. It was five minutes past three. In the morning that is. The man in the grey suit lay there. His body made small, quiet convulsive movements for about three minutes. I felt myself timing them. Nobody went to his assistance. Blood formed a darkening patch on his suit. If you blinked every time you opened your eyes again there was more dark liquid, there. It didn't seem to be flowing from anywhere. It's just that the stain kept getting bigger. The blood had trouble soaking into the carpet and dispersing. A pool was following; it was getting deeper. You could see that this man was badly hurt.

Lenny turned around in his seat. He made that blowing noise again. 'Phoooooooow. This is serious stuff. I can't believe I'm sitting here watching this as calm as you like.'

The man was lying there still bleeding. The stain spreading. His movements were becoming slighter and quieter. 'Oh fuck,' I said. It sounded like a fabricated emotion the first time. Not quite right. I remember that I had that thought, that observation of my own behaviour at that precise moment in that slowed down, elongated interval.

'Fuck, fuck, fuck,' I said louder this time. It sounded more genuine like that, it needed that intensity to come out more like how I felt. 'Is he dead?' I looked at Big Lenny. 'Is he dead?' I said it again to get some response. 'How do you know when he's dead, Lenny?' I let my voice rise higher this time, begging him to come in. Begging. 'Is that it?' I could hear my voice full of emotion now, as if it had somehow got there itself in the end, but I was now trying to control it. Lenny just sat there immobile, transfixed.

'I can't believe we just sat through all that.' I could hear my voice now as if it wasn't me who was doing the talking.

'He's a goner alright,' said Big Lenny eventually. 'He's well gone.'

'Did you see it coming?' I asked. The question came out very rushed. More rushed than I had intended. He didn't answer. He was still watching. I tried speaking more slowly to see if that would help. 'Could you see it coming?' This time I put pauses between all the words, and emphasized the word 'it'. The question emerged with a staccato rhythm, like stones tapping a window with a light tap, tap, tap.

The man in the stained suit was quite still now. Death right in front of us, with no words that we could hear. A life terminated in and through silent action. Hardly any words had been spoken at all between the protagonists. It was life and death negotiated through the silent language of the body. That was the scary thing.

Lenny and I were still stationary in our seats. 'I could see something,' said Lenny. 'But I didn't think that it would be a knife in the belly like that. So much blood. I can't get over the amount of blood that comes out of a belly. Look at that carpet. It will cost a fortune to get that clean. Look at the mess. Who owns this place? Do you know who actually owns the club? He's not going to be very pleased when he turns up. It will cost him a fortune to get the whole thing cleaned.'

I almost laughed to hear Big Lenny talking about the dry cleaning bill after what we had just witnessed. Perhaps it was his way of dealing with it. On the other hand, perhaps he really cared about these sorts of things. I got up and pulled out my hanky and wiped my forehead. I was feeling hot, as if I had been out for a short fast run. My heart was beating quickly. I think that I had seen enough. I looked at Lenny. He was still watching the man lying on the floor. I couldn't remember the man's name. I had been told it, I just couldn't remember it. I had made no effort to remember it. It would have made the whole thing too personal, I suppose. He was just the man in the grey suit. A man whose hand had wandered in a sleazy after-hours drinking club, or a man who had been playing away with somebody else's girlfriend, depending upon your point of view, depending upon how much you were prepared to read into things.

Lenny saw me looking this time. He tried a smile. 'I can't believe this. I didn't think it would be quite like this. It's funny if you're not involved in things. It seems different. I wouldn't stab somebody anyway. It's not my style, I'll tell you that for nothing.' Then he went silent, as if he might be thinking.

There was silence in that room. I felt myself sniffing and it sounded loud. Just enough to break the solemn silence.

'Can we play that last bit again,' said Lenny. 'That last section. Can we rewind the tape and then I might pick up a bit more? Just one more time.'

I said that he could watch the whole thing again if he wanted to, and I leaned back in my seat glad that it was all over. He leant across to the video-recorder and pressed the rewind button. The tape whining into action almost made me jump. 'You might be a man worth knowing after all,' he said. 'Not such a Muppet head, as I first thought,' and he winked over at me and nodded.

'I can't believe that you get to watch this sort of stuff for a living, Mr. Psychologist, that's a nice little perk for you and your friends.' And he leaned back in his chair, and spread his legs, deliberately and provocatively, taking up all of the available space in that small viewing room in the social psychology suite of the university, establishing his territory, reminding me of his dominance position, pushing me into the corner both physically and symbolically.

'I'm pleased that you invited me along to help out with your analysis,' he said grinning. 'I'll let you know what my fee is for my consultancy work here, and ...,' he added, 'we could also do a nice little rental on this snuff movie here to make a few extra quid.'

I explained to him, my voice full of anxiety and hesitation, that

I had signed all sorts of legal documents that I would keep the video-tape completely confidential and that I had agreed that nobody else, under any circumstances, would be allowed to view this tape. It was only to be viewed by me in my capacity as a potential expert witness on body language in an upcoming court case.

'That's your problem, boss, not mine,' was his reply. And he gave me a great relaxed wink and I swear that he licked his lips for the second time that night.

# THREE

I had been in Sheffield for just over a year at this point. I had wanted to live in the North for my own reasons. I wanted to live among the mines and the steel works and the ordinary people without the airs and graces that I had been putting up with for the past three years down in Cambridge. I knew that it was hard up North. I had heard all about the redundancies and the unemployment. An economic desert, my college tutor had called it, questioning why I wanted to move there exactly. I had my reasons, I said. Perhaps I wanted to help the ordinary people in the last great stand of the working class. Perhaps, I was that idealistic at that time. I don't know now.

The day of the move will always stick in my mind. At least, parts of it will. You never remember everything. Any psychologist could tell you that. There are different types of memory. Memories for faces, memories for names, semantic memory, memories for events. Flashbulb memories where the mind opens up and lets it all flood in, every detail and nuance of the scene saved for all time. That day I think I had several flashbulb memories, flashbulbs of hot glass that burned in my mind an indelible image. It was that important to me.

It was autumn, and then this was the first thing I really noticed that day on the drive North. I mean really noticed. I saw it coming up in the distance, but even from that oblique angle I could recognize it. It meant something, as my mind did the necessary computations to turn it from a pattern of lines and geometric shapes into something suffused with meaning and significance. I could feel my excitement rise. I was getting close. It was like crossing a border. It was silhouetted against an iron grey sky. It was quite flat, a sharp outline, and two dimensional like a picture. Self-contained, framed by green fields with muddy tracks through them leading into the distance. Flat, dark features against a grey October background. Old strangely familiar shapes. Shapes from my past, inculcated by *his* stories and tales and the odd picture from a book. Shapes that I know ended up in a multitude of disguises in my dreams. Spoked wheels of fire, rectangular metal cages that descend into hell, fire and brimstone. Shapes that he had spoken about, and described.

This was the source of many of the images out of which the flowing narrative of my dreams were made. But I suspect that the real source was not the object now in front of me but his telling of it, his version of the industrial North, his version of that coal mine over there in the middle of that muddy field, and what that mine meant to him and therefore what it should mean to me.

Sometimes I laughed about the fact that he even controlled my dreams. The mine in my dream with all its convoluted symbolism looked much more real than here in real life. As I looked closer, I could see that the real mine was untidier than in any pictures I had seen or any images that I ever had provided for me. There were more bits and pieces left around the place. More debris. More mess. There were wagons parked, probably containers waiting to be loaded. But they were carelessly parked. They almost looked abandoned. So this is the North, I thought to myself.

Then I had this one thought. He would have seen it like this on his first day travelling north to Yorkshire, past the pits of Nottinghamshire. The silhouette, the familiarity, the flatness, even the untidiness that had not been anticipated.

That was the thought that was at the forefront of my mind

that autumn day. My eyes were seeing it for the first time. Just as his had done once. We were united again. Briefly. I noticed that I had goose bumps extending along both arms, and separately outwards along the cheeks of my face. It wasn't in any way a profound thought; it was just emotion. It was just my body reacting to an emotional message from within itself.

I had slipped out of Cambridge earlier that day. It had been one of those golden autumny sort of days, before the greyness of a Fenland winter, as I left with all of my worldly possessions packed into my little brown Triumph Spitfire. My suitcase that would not close, my sleeping bag unfurling in front of me, my rucksack, which was not designed for any Alpine peak, not quite fastened, a large green screen print of an almost human figure on a Martian landscape, painted by an art school friend, blocking the back window, two briefcases - one leather and one a poor shiny vinyl on the seat beside me slipping and sliding at every turn. I was virtually invisible in the middle of all my clutter.

My friends from my college lodgings had lined up to wave me off. Nobody shook hands. You could see that it was on their minds though, their hands flapped by their sides invitingly. I never responded. The landlady presented me with some shortbread, and she passed the tin in through the side window and stroked my shoulder by way of farewell. Two short abrupt strokes along the top of my shoulder signaled good-bye to my varsity days.

I drove out past Fitzwilliam and then Girton, past students with long, slender tanned legs in still flimsy skirts, legs tanned in late holidays in Thailand or Phuket, cycling in for lectures at the very start of the new academic year. All were travelling in the opposite direction to me.

I gazed longingly at these fresh new buds in this seasonal town, buds as bright as those seen in any spring, buds waiting to burst open in the weeks and months ahead. Autumn, the season that would deepen into weeks of Fenland mist, was really our spring - just as fresh and just as exciting. Summer was our long winter, barren and bare, except for the tourists cramming King's Parade, obstacles on the road to pass on my bicycle on the way to the department. Nuisances who swarmed onto the road and got in the way of your bicycle, and packed the coffee shops late in the afternoon when you needed some break from your work.

You would see them trying to punt on the Cam waving and shouting. You could hear them splashing and giggling under the bridges on the Backs as you cycled home at night in the summer evenings.

Cambridge wasn't for me punts and strawberries and King's Chapel at night. It was days spent living in the Gothic darkness of the Downing Site where many of the science departments were situated. I spent my time in tall, dark, brooding buildings with dusty staircases which, unlike the colleges, invited no strangers to enter. It was weeks spent on experiments that had a life of their own, and had to be tended to keep them alive and functioning through those barren months of summer, when the rest of the world seemed to be having such gay distracting fun almost within ear shot.

But this was all at an end now. The time had come to spread our academic wings, to move on, my tutor had said. We were all moving on - Harward, Heidelberg, UCL, Stanford, MIT ... Sheffield. It was pot luck for most, jobs gained on hearsay and academic reputation, which can be a flimsy thing especially at that age, but my journey was more planned than most.

I was driving away from Cambridge, until there was no more sight of those long, golden limbs on bicycles. I passed green fields that were empty and quiet apart from the caw, caw, cawing of crows in the copses of trees, and later I passed Happy Eaters and Little Chefs and traffic that flowed and ebbed and eventually tapered onto a single line north. It was now raining, with a great swash of rain running down the windscreen.

I slowed down. A lorry overtook me, and the spray covered my windscreen with a heavy splosh of dirty water. I watched the wipers struggle to dislodge the mass of muddy water streaking my windscreen. But I needed to take my eyes off the road, to look again at that wheel out there. I wanted to freeze that percept before it was too late, and to store that image intact, so that I would be able to evoke it at will, and then we would be together in the realm of sensation whenever I wished.

But I had to watch the road and the percept kept changing significantly with every movement of the wiper blades and every yard the car travelled. The changing percept would make the memory fuzzy and therefore vague and useless.

I clung to the thought instead. Just the abstract thought. These were two pairs of eyes that belonged together, and here was the same vista at different times. Just different times, that's all. It was a union of sorts, a coming together. It was the thought that excited me. That could not be taken away. I could sense him beside me, seeing the mine, feeling what I was feeling, thinking similar thoughts. That was how desperate I was at that time, coming to terms with my brother's death.

He had died in an accident almost exactly one year before, and there had not been one night where I had not seen him briefly in my dreams. At first he would talk to me, and we would walk together through strange and unfamiliar landscapes, but recently he seemed always to be walking away from me, or leaving buildings that I was just entering. And in those buildings somewhere there would be cages and wheels and sometimes fire and the closing curtains of blackness. Sometimes there was to be no comfort.

My mother missed him badly, and whenever I was back home and the room smelt heavy of whisky, she would often burst into great gulps of lugubrious, self-pitying tears that took her breath away. You could see her reaching out for the glass that had been knocked over, lying on its side up against the settee. The whisky soaking into the red swirly carpet that now had a smell all its own, like a pub late in the afternoon, behind drawn curtains. If you pressed the carpet down hard enough, you could squeeze stale drink out of it from the previous night's lonely rituals.

My father had died years before, I can hardly remember him, he even looks unfamiliar in his photographs now, and so my mother was quite alone in her grief. She told me that I was no help to a widow woman. She liked the sound of those words. Widow woman. My brother would have been more help to her. She made me feel this without saying it directly. And now he had been taken from her.

I wanted to tell her that he had also been taken from me, but I don't think that she would have been that interested. I would try to talk with her as she drank, and I would see her glance at me, a glance as vague and as grey and unformed as twilight. A glance that never seemed to connect with anything within me.

So she lay there, drinking and sobbing, saying his name over and over again, as if it might help to talk. Waiting up for him through the night, like you would wait for a lover. Sometimes, you could hear what sounded like real conversations with her part of the conversation shaped and sculpted for all the social demands of dialogue. You could hear her voice rising to ask questions and sometimes you could hear the downward intonation of an assertion appearing in her voice as if she was telling him what he must do. Perhaps, she was warning him. She left gaps in her speech, as if he might be answering back. I don't know if she heard his replies. I never listened that carefully. I didn't want to intrude.

One night I had come in late and found her up, lying in front of the television, still on despite the fact that the programs had finished hours ago. The crackling set illuminated her face. She was half asleep and came to slowly, annoyed to be woken up so late, or so early. She started to sit up. She was half asleep and started talking to me. She told me through those bleary eyes that she wished it had been me who had slipped off that mountain side that day. She wished that it was me who had plunged that fine bright morning in snow-covered Nepal into the hallowed sanctity of pontifical death.

But it was just the drink talking. That's what they say, isn't it? Just the drink talking, as if the drink could conceptualize such hurt, and plan such complex syntactic structures, and articulate all on its own. Just the drink talking?

I don't think so.

In the morning I am sure that she never remembered saying any of this. She told me that she must have fallen asleep in the living room, as she tried to clean up. She was rubbing furiously at the carpet. There was something that had to be erased from the night before. She, at least, knew that.

It was never mentioned again, never returned to. But she had sobbed it out at me that night, like it was the painful truth, like it was hard to say. She may not have remembered it afterwards, but I can remember every word and every nuance of pause for breath and for emphasis, and every nuance of tone in that short sobbing sentence. I had stored this sentence intact as some kind of articulatory loop for my memory, to play back to myself, to use as a weapon against myself or against her, depending on how I felt.

My mother sought to find my brother in old tear-stained photographs, where he had a gap in his teeth and thick eyebrows, in the days before she started plucking them. She always tended him when he was a boy, plucking his eyebrows, fixing his tie, smoothing his hair. I never got that attention. She said that I didn't need it. My tie was always straight and my eyebrows managed to grow in quite a controlled way all on their own, without any intervention.

They were very close. I enjoyed my own company. That's what everybody said, especially my mother. I was always a bit *odd* when I was young, she said, a bit private. That's what she meant by 'odd', just more private than most. She didn't mean 'peculiar', she just meant that I could do without the constant distracting hum of social interaction when I was a child, if I had to.

I would take my scooter every night up to the top park gate, regardless of the weather or the season, and count the strides in the rain or the mist to get to the third railing past the gate, the one with the rust covering its base. I would try to take exact strides on the way up, with strides of exactly the same length and exactly the same pressure on the ground with my right shoe to keep the number constant. That was my goal on the outward journey - consistency. I suppose now I would call it consistency in measurement. Numbers that matched.

I would even wear the same shoes night after night so that this would not be a variable in this difficult equation. And not just night after night, but year after year, my mother and I would have constant battles about these shoes. She never understood the significance of those black, cracked leather shoes with the rounded toes, which she was always trying to throw out. But they were critical in the mathematics of the whole thing. Critical to the consistency. She would never have understood any of this. She thought that they were just shabby, just worn out and fit for the bin.

I would push myself up to that spike, then I would time myself to the bottom gate with the second hand of my watch. I never raced anybody. Nobody else would have been much interested in a race from one arbitrary spike to another, a distance of four hundred and ten to four hundred and twelve scooter strides. I was competing against myself on the way back. That was what mattered. And checking to make sure that my estimates of distance and speed and pressure on the way up were accurate.

Sometimes I think that I was made for Cambridge. Made for Cambridge. It sounds strange for me to say that. But I don't mean the Cambridge that springs to mind so readily. The Cambridge of punts or strawberries or May Balls, or other fragments like that, but the other Cambridge - the Cambridge behind the screen. The Cambridge of long quiet nights spent in my room at the top of what used to be the Cold Temperature Building, with John in the next room. John the man who never spoke except when you forced him. John who worked all through the night perfecting his psychophysical measurement techniques. Often still there in the mornings, looking a little disheveled and a little confused.

John had very poor social skills and didn't like greetings or partings or anything else that involved ritualized social behaviour, especially if it also involved human physical contact. The touch. He hated the freezing necessity of the touch, and the way that most of the rituals of life pulled you towards it, or involved it in some devious way. He just liked shuffling through life in his own, idiosyncratic manner. He didn't like public transport, especially trains, and as he couldn't drive his life was a little constrained by distance and travel. Cambridge was in many ways perfect for him. He never had to go anywhere else, or bump into strangers or greet them or touch them.

I think that he may still be there now, still in a room on the top floor of the building, still working on psychophysical laws applied to all the senses. All the senses except touch, that is. Too complicated, he would say. Far too complicated, even for us.

That Cambridge.

I wasn't like John. I was never quite like that. I never minded social contact even when I was a child, but I was just choosier than most. I didn't crave interaction like some people, who are nothing without it. Their only meanings in life come from other's response to them. There is no internal meaning. When they are on their own their life seems empty. My brother needed friends around him, all of the time. So did my mother. That was why she was so desolate on her own now.

My brother and his friends would sometimes watch me on my scooter at night up by the park, under the street lights where the bats would flap and swoop at criss-crossing angles through the black night air. Occasionally, he and his friends would hear me riding along, counting out loud the number of strides on my routine out and back. I didn't want to lose count. If I did I would have to start all over again and go back right to the beginning. They would all laugh at me, including my brother. He wouldn't try to defend me. That hurt me deeply.

Sometimes, he would lay his hanky out on the park railings because he said he had heard that it attracted bats. The park keeper had told him that. He didn't want to study the bats, he just wanted his friends to get close enough to them to at least touch them with their sticks. A violent touch, of course, but it was the touch rather than the violence that was crucial. The touch would be a demonstration that my brother and his friends were in control, evidence that they understood how bats could be drawn down from their meaningless zig-zagging forays across the blackened night sky.

A dead bat would have been even better. That would be a permanent demonstration of their success, of their superiority in this regard. But they never came near to that. There was never any waxy, festering bat carcass to look at in our house. None that I can remember anyway.

They would all be standing there, waiting for a bat to come in low, and I would be passing by, having to go round them, and having to change my route and my distance to make allowances for them. Counting out, counting aloud. I would be counting again and again, pass after pass, and they would be just standing there, laughing as I got near, keeping their loudest guffaws to the precise moment when I passed. I thought it was his friends who were funny, with their pathetic understanding of the perceptual system of the bat, who managed to avoid the acoustic ripples emanating outwards from this little huddle with their sticks swishing aimlessly though the night air.

After he died, my mother would sit with these old photographs of my brother on her lap, smoothing down the corners, dog-eared from the wet teastained caresses. She was still tending him as she had always done. I had left for university and a life away from the two of them, I missed many of the one-sided conversations that went on throughout the night. And for that I was very grateful. But in the vacations I would sometimes find myself travelling to places where he had once lived. I always had some good reason for this. New friends from college who just happened to know these places - Lancaster, Sheffield, the North. Places he had been and talked about. I had images of Stocksbridge and Dungworth, Glossop and Stannage Edge. Romantic images.

Perhaps I just wanted to see if they lived up to their image. Like that coal mine in front of me. Or perhaps, I was trying to find him. The way that you might walk back along the pavement looking for a penny that has dropped out of your pocket. You would never admit to it, but you might take the detour past where it had fallen out of your pocket, just in case it was still there. I know that I would anyway. I couldn't rest until I found it. I need order, you see. I need everything in its place.

Perhaps, I secretly thought that he might have left part of himself behind in these dark Northern places, part of his spirit might be found wandering in the places where he had lived. I might even be able to feel close to him in those dark Northern hills.

It's quite funny, because at one time I was glad to get away from him, now I wanted to get some of him back, perhaps just so that order in my life could be restored. Perhaps, it was just because I hate loose ends. I was who I was partly as a reaction against him. We are all reactions against something. The opposite of 'modelling' I suppose, the opposite of copying or imitation. We decide what we do not want to become. Without him, I could become many different things, perhaps too many different things.

Perhaps *even* him.

My travels in the North were like a pilgrim's journey. Sometimes I didn't know if I was doing it for me or for my mother. I would ring her up just to say hello, and tell her that I was in Lancaster, and for a moment she would be confused as to which son it was that was calling her so late at night. Sometimes she called me Phil by mistake. I didn't bother correcting her. I let her have a conversation with her other son for a change. I thought that it might do her some good. I thought that it might be good for her to have her son back for a while. You could hear her coming round on the phone, her mind slowly trying to remember what it was that was blackening and shading her days. She would sound shaken, a little confused. Sometimes I thought that she was getting confused more generally, stuck in that room day-in, day-out with the dog-eared photographs and the swirly red carpet.

I, on the other hand, wanted to move on with my life, to leave all this mourning behind. I was sure that he would have been proud of me now, travelling to my first job in Sheffield, with the rock faces of Stannage Edge on the edge of the city, with his impression perhaps still on the wet grey millstone grit slabs. I was the only academic one of the family, and I was going there to lecture at the university. He said that he was too pretty to study and whenever he worked in our bedroom he told us that he would have to dismantle the mirror on the dresser so that he would not be distracted by his own image. He never went to university. He said that there were more important things in life than reading books and thinking old thoughts and hearing familiar arguments that took you inexorably to conclusions that you could have antic-ipated without any of the unnecessary grind. More to life than the jiggling and twisting of old ideas. I would just smile at this rea-soning. I knew that he really didn't believe it. He was cleverer than that.

I looked out at the mine with the sticky looking mounds of the blackest coal heaped beside it, just fifty yards or so from the road. The windscreen wipers tic tocced across my view. He saw that same image. He would have kept it in his mind. The image would have fired his imagination. You could imagine the black souls toiling in the darkness underneath. He would have sensed their toil. That's a term he liked - 'sense'. He liked intuition and feeling and sensing things, the untutored art and the untaught skills of being a human being. He would have had an intuitive understanding of the nature of their toil.

He had never *really* worked. But that's what he liked to talk about. The nobility of the working-man in his struggle to survive, the class struggle, the miners. Always the miners. He was there at Orgreave with them during the miners' strike. He faced the police on horseback. He told me about rolling a tyre at the police line. It was all his idea. That's what he said. I saw it on *News at Ten*. The tire rolling down the hillside gathering pace, the police scattering in its wake. I never saw Phil though. He was probably too clever to be captured on video by *News at Ten*. Far too clever for that.

He loved Orgreave. He told me about the feeling of being part of something greater for the first time in his life. Part of something with some meaning. Arms locked with the miners in a fight to the finish for their very survival. Class war. He described it all a lot better than me. I've tried before. I make it sound like I'm reading from a pamphlet. He said it all as if it was new, as if it was all his idea.

Class war. That's a laugh. We weren't really any class. We couldn't fight *for* any class; we couldn't fight *against* any class. We were both born into a family that somehow fell between classes. We were skilled working class, I suppose, and then my father went and got a job in a technical college, but as a technician. We didn't feel that protective solidarity of the real working-class or benefit from the smug complacency of the middle-class.

When I can wield images like this, it tells you something about the distance of our family from both classes. After all, it's harder to generalize about groups when you are part of them. Up close to anything, you just see diversity and difference. I, on the other hand, sitting viewing social class from our great distance just saw homogeneity and similarity. We were nothing really. I went to university and Phil set off on his adventures, wherever his fancy took him, like a nineteenth-century adventurer with a private income. And I definitely don't know what it made my mother, still stuck in the same old house. But according to Mrs. Thatcher we were all middle class now anyway, so none of it should have mattered. But it did.

My brother said we were working class because my father worked and then we struggled after his death. It was a struggle to keep our family together, he said.

Since my brother's death our social class had become even more confused. It was enough for my mother to get through to morning without worrying what others might think. There was nothing genteel about her conversations with my dead brother. She would swear and rage at him into the early hours. She did not care what anybody thought. There was no mask of gentility or pretence.

The rain was coming down heavier now. I could hardly see the mine. I was thinking that this might have been where he first saw a mine, a real mine.

I could feel the energy of the place for myself. Just as he had described in his letters. You can feel the energy coming to the surface from a coal mine, like an earthquake starting deep in the earth. There was an energy here. I think that I could see the pit village in the background, although it was very misty and my windscreen was dirty. I closed my eyes and thought of him, walking away seven years before when I was still at school, walking down our little road in search of his adventure, in search of the common man in Thatcher's Britain. In search of all this.

The thought exhilarated me. I felt that we were together again. Me and him, and me and them. Those in the belly of the earth, toiling for hours underground. And me up here in the driving rain, toiling for hours along the A1.

He was always walking away. His walk is one of the easiest things for me to recall about him. I just have to close my eyes and there it is. It was a little lop-sided walk, lower on the left for some reason, with a real spring in his step as if he was floating above the ground. I can only visualize him and his walk that clearly from the back though.

It's funny that. He always seemed to be walking away from me, never coming towards me. I sensed that he enjoyed that sweet sorrow of parting. He liked partings, quite unlike my neighbour, John, from the Low Temperature Building. It made him feel wanted. He liked hugs and caresses and my mother's tears.

I hated those tears.

He liked engineering farewells. He never stayed anywhere too long. He left the miners to pursue other great adventures. Climbing great sharp, jagged rocks, scaling snow-covered mountains that petered out somewhere in the clouds above some distant, foreign land. Even death itself would be an adventure for him. But that's such a cliché it's difficult to say.

I was getting near my destination, so I wanted to observe everything now. I wanted to take everything in. Even the twists and turns of the road, anything that he himself would have seen. The low grey sky, the rain coming in at an angle, the muddied fields battered by these harsh forces. Not the litter or the burnt-out joyrider's car at the side of the road with the blackened wheels on the melted tarmac. Not those. Those were too new. I wanted a sense of history and a sense of place and a sense of my brother.

He introduced me to Engels. Sheffield in the last century. 'The worker comes home tired and exhausted from his labours. He finds that his comfortless and unattractive dwelling is both damp and dirty. He urgently needs some stimulant; he must have something to recompense him for his labours during the day and enable him to face the prospect of the next day's dreary toil.'

'Recompense'. I loved the way that he said that word. He always looked at me on the last syllable, as if to emphasize it, as if to send me a special message. It was the start of his political period. 'Pense'. It sounded like 'pence', but was spelt like 'pensee'. He was clever, using homophonic reference to stir my imagination in this way. Think, he was saying. Think about money and capitalism, and how the petit bourgeoisie, hold up the class system. You'll be one of them one day.'

I was always going to turn into 'the petit bourgeoisie' when it suited him. Think about all of this. Think about what we must do. I looked out and the mine had gone.

I drove along quietly now. The landscape was changing again. He would have noticed this. Then I saw it, coming into view. Rows of terraced housing on grey hills out in front of me. Giant blocks of flats appearing from nowhere. A city built on seven hills, like the Eternal City, all the terraced houses looping around meandering hills at the end of the dual carriageway.

The road was stopping quite abruptly, expiring right in the heart of the Northern city by the flats that dominated the view. Castles in the sky. That's what he called them sometimes. Castles in the sky or prison ships, it depended on his mood sometimes, and what he was reading.

So this was it. This was the great mythical North that I had dreamt of back in Cambridge.

But he would have pulled into this lane and had to break in that same kind of way as me. We were one again. I drove around the roundabout twice, unable to find my exit. A car tooted at me. I could feel myself reddening with embarrassment. My left hand rose in a placatory sort of gesture. I mouthed 'sorry'. I'm new here, new to the North, I tried to explain, in that instant of distant contact. The car drove right up behind me. I could see the driver giving me the fingers as he took the next left. I waved back. I know that it was a stupid gesture, but it was automatic. I knew that he hadn't waved at me. I just couldn't stop myself. It was like an unconditioned response, well perhaps not unconditioned, it might have been conditioned slightly by years of polite existence back home. He made a kind of waving movement, so I waved back. Even though his wave involved just two fingers. Whatever system one has for detecting and responding to movements of this kind couldn't discriminate the fingers quick enough. At least mine couldn't.

I had to find my way to my digs. I followed the signs to the university, and passed an exhaust garage on the left. It was on the map that the university had sent to me. The exhaust garage was represented by a little drawing in red. 'Pass it on the left,' the map said. It was then that I saw her.

I pulled up at some lights and she was standing on the pavement. I thought that she was waiting for a bus. She dipped her head in a smooth, practiced swing so that she could look in, but without really seeing me. It was as if she wanted her eyes to be at the right level to make contact. I assumed that she wanted to ask me for some directions. I was starting to prepare 'I'm sorry, I'm a stranger here too', ready for when I got the window down. The only problem was that it always stuck. I was trying to get the window down. She suddenly straightened up as if to say 'It doesn't matter.'

She didn't actually say that, but her nonverbal communication said it - her posture, her gesture, even her facial expression. I had been studying nonverbal communication of these types for the past three years for my doctorate - body language in popular parlance. Not necessarily female body language, but body language more generally. I mean that I study the code rather than the person, which is the way that I think it should be.

Body language without the actual body, if you like. That's what I was an expert on.

# FOUR

Perhaps, I need to explain what I mean a little more carefully. I mean that I spent most of my three years of research studying hand gestures without noticing the calluses on the hand or the dirt behind the nails or the size of the middle finger, that's what I mean. I studied students trying to find certain words that they knew but couldn't quite articulate. That's a big part of what I had been doing for the past three years, sitting people like myself, well not exactly like myself because I wouldn't actually have volunteered, down in my experimental room in Cambridge and reading them definitions of words and video-recording them whilst their mind tried to find the word concerned. I was inducing a tip-of-the-tongue state and I studied in great slow-motion detail the operation of their mind, and more significantly their body, as they attempted to resolve it.

I was interested, you see, in their nonverbal communication, their communication beyond words, whilst they grimaced and grappled and gestured for those words whose definitions I read to them.

I watched their gestures in slow motion, and noted every twist and turn, and every tiny flutter and movement as the hands articulated in front of me in that musty room in Cambridge with the egg boxes covering the walls for extra sound-proofing.

This is why I analyzed students stunned by their own silence

GEOFFREY BEATTIE

in that sound-proof room, a room that reflected silence back at you, a room that magnified every millisecond of silence opening up in the mean trickle of speech coming out of your mouth, producing great, deep lakes of nothingness into which the speaker could easily fall and die.

One particular student was certain that he knew the word for 'the instrument used for measuring angles on paper'. But he couldn't quite find the word immediately, when put on the spot in that musty room with some hidden camera pointing at him. He was not a psychology student, and it made him slightly anxious to be in their presence. I watched that confidence of his, confidence bred into him over generations, falter slightly in that musty experimental room. Anxiety can block most of the mental operations that are necessary for speech, like sand in an engine.

He just couldn't find the right word, and got quite desperate in front of me.

'Oh … it's a … it's ah ah … a circumference thing … I know what it is … it's that bloody arc thing … oh no what's the bloody word?'

You could hear him getting annoyed at himself. First the anxiety, and then the anger. I would watch all this in slow motion and freeze the frames, and note the facial expression of self-directed anger forming in front of me. The lip curl, the eyes tightening and then closing, the hissing sometimes that went along with it.

'It's on the tip-of-my-tongue. It's … um … circumferential. Oh shit excuse me. It's erm … ar- arch ro- ro- is it … r-r-r-. Oh God! Oh God! Something … ah … ah … arc arch … um rotor arc.'

It was quite pathetic to listen to sometimes, if I'm totally honest. The pleading, the vague attempts at an answer, the um's and ah's appearing out of the frozen silence of the speech, like huge icebergs, only the tips of all that frustrating search showing in the talk itself, and the speaker foundering on these malevolent, brooding physical objects that now blocked his path.

I don't know if I would have been any better in the situation, but I never had to put myself through it.

I watched the hands, without any conscious deliberation or planning, preparing themselves, moving quickly and quite unconsciously into the right area in front of the body, the fingers starting to take shape. Then, as he tried to find the word 'protractor', I watched his right hand making a semi-circular movement quickly, with the index finger pointing outwards, with the left hand moving only slightly. Then I watched his right hand and his left hand moving quickly around each other five times in circular fashion, five times in all the hands represented that shape with the fingers bent in but with the index fingers pointing outwards. It was all there, and yet I could see in every frame of his facial expression that he couldn't quite get it.

I watched these gestures again and again map out iconically the critical feature of the particular word he was searching for - the semi-circular shape of the object, even though he never managed to locate this word in his mental lexicon.

In other words, I watched his body take precedence over his mind in his accessing of his internal mental store. I watched the body get there first, when the mind couldn't quite articulate what it was searching for. I watched his hand gestures spell out the single most significant semantic property of the word 'protractor', when his mind completely failed to find the word among the thousands of other entries in his mental store.

Eventually, after a long pause at the very end of his predetermined misery period he offered me the word 'compass', but he knew it was wrong. I could see it in every frame of his face. So could the video-camera behind the one-way mirror, poking through the egg boxes, watching his every frozen movement.

It was just frustration on my subject's part. He had to offer me something. He couldn't find the word 'protractor'. He couldn't just say nothing. His body knew that it was the wrong word. His body had got it right. His body knew the shape of the object 'pro-tractor' and his hands had traced out all of the critical angles inherent in that object. A compass had none of these angles.

I studied all of this without once noticing the individual warts or cuts or moles on the hands. We were all alike under the skin. All frustrated and angry with the inner workings of our minds whilst our bodies worked and worked and worked away almost without us, almost in spite of us.

It was all about body language without an actual body inside.

I talked to my brother excitedly about iconic hand movement the last time I saw him. I told him all about the metaphoric prop-erties of human movement as it articulates itself in space and configures complex shapes that we all understand without con-scious reflection or deliberation. He looked at me with that gleam in his eye. That gleam. It was his look. His eyes had a sparkle about them. Bright eyes that caught the light and shone the light right back at you. Not like the eyes I studied in the laboratory. They were dull and bored or anxious and terrified, nervy, flitting this way and that as if they were having secret insecure thoughts that they were trying desperately to conceal from me. It was funny that. His eyes were never like the ones that I viewed under my microscope.

'Why are you doing this sort of stuff?' he asked 'Eye gaze, mutual gaze, iconic bollocks.' He laughed until he cried, until the tears rolled down his face. But I loved the sound that he made when he laughed like that. I loved that laugh, even when he was laughing at me. When I was younger I would say stupid things just to make him laugh out loud like that. Stupid but plausible things. Things that I really might have meant. In church he had explained to me all about Advent and Epiphany and Lent and how these periods were reflected in the crimsons and golds on the pulpit. So I asked him what colour the church used for Halloween, and he laughed so loudly that the woman behind asked us both to shut up or leave. The next Sunday I asked him the same question again, the very same words, hoping for the same response. But it didn't work the second time around.

Perhaps, he thought that I was trying to elicit another laugh by talking about my work, just another laugh. I will never know now. I will never ever know now and that makes me very sad indeed.

I was still trying to get the window down. She had stepped back. I saw her skirt for the first time and her long thin white legs without tights. I hadn't noticed these before. The skirt was very short. She had big black bruises, which had started to turn blue, on her pencil thin white legs. 'Hi,' I said, 'can I help you?'

'What?' she said in reply. She was frowning heavily. She was quite pretty, but her eyebrows were knotted. There were deep creases across her forehead.

'Um, can I help you in some way?'

'What are you fucking on about?' she said.

I could feel myself going red. First the tooting and now this. People only tooted at me about once a month, and as for this! Everyone back at university was so pleasant to each other, even when they were pretending to be so distant that they hardly recognized you. They were still cordial, even with their studied indifference.

'Would you like some directions or something?' I said. I guessed that she didn't want directions, but I couldn't think of anything else to ask. I felt that I had to ask something rather than tell her something.

'Fuck off,' she said, and she turned her back and walked off.

I could feel that gesture starting again. That wave of mine. I was signalling, but to nobody in particular.

She glanced back at me. 'Go fuck yourself, you time wasting twat.'

'Okay,' I said quietly, almost inaudibly. 'Thank you.'

So this is the North, I said to myself. I'm finally here.

# FIVE

I was looking for the house in which I was to lodge. 'Edelweiss' it had said on the letter I had received from the landlady. I'd laughed when I saw the name. It was an Alpine flower whose image I could not conjure up in my mind, and an old song whose tune I unfortunately couldn't get out of my head.

'Edelweiss, Edelweiss.' I repeated those words over and over again, but I couldn't remember any of the other words of the song. I thought of Alpine peaks and him beneath the ground, beneath that deep Nepal snow. And I thought of the seasons changing around him, and the snow melting.

'Edelweiss, Edelweiss.' I guessed that there would probably be white mountain flowers in the Spring out in Nepal, erupting though the brown earth, made damp with the snows melting. And I imagined him lying there quite still, not motionless but quite still, a stillness like sleep. A contented sort of sleep. I would work my way down along his body from his hair freshly washed, always freshly washed, with traces of freshly turned soil, down over his orange climbing jacket billowing outwards to those treacherous boots that had slipped on ice wet rock. But I imagined that jacket growing looser and looser over the years although I never wanted to peep inside.

These were powerful images which I tried to control. Unsuccessfully. But that is the ultimate legacy of death I suppose, areas of the mind and areas of consciousness become out of bounds. If you stray in accidentally you stick in the sucking quag-mires of longing and dread. Conscious thought becomes a treacherous journey, the mind becomes a strange and dangerous land with narrow paths to be navigated with great care at all times.

The house was university-approved accommodation. It was on a road behind some shops. That will be handy, I had thought to myself when I saw the map with all the possible lodgings sketched in, if I run out of food late at night. That was why I had picked it, I suppose. It was a mundane enough reason.

I had an image of what it was going to be like there. I saw myself in some airy attic, impossibly airy, in fact. Air coming in from all sides. High in the white light, overlooking some recog-nizable view, a dark mill perhaps, Northern, dark fumes pouring into the night sky, the paper in front of me, the paper always white, always waiting for me.

I drove along until I found the road. It was a hilly tree-lined road, a bit more run-down than I had imagined from the sketch map the university had provided. I couldn't find the right number because the hedges were so over-grown, so I parked my car and walked along the road. It had stopped raining now.

There was a gang of lads on the corner, smoking and cursing and pushing each other. Sixteen or seventeen, perhaps. I'm not very good at guessing ages. They always look older than they are. I guess it's the way they live. I missed out on that life really. I was too busy studying.

Missed out, that's a funny choice of words here. How can you miss out on that?

Those boring, idle rituals of the night, swearing and cursing and smoking and fingering girls up dark alleys. I was too busy studying for my 'A' levels, working hard to get - well - here where I am today - with them in that same road. No, that sounds ridicu-lous. I wasn't with them. I was moving through here, moving up, moving past them on my career trajectory. They were stuck here.

They weren't going anywhere, and they knew it.

I could hear their loud communal laughter. Then they went quiet. Together. A dirty story or some other tale pulling them all into that dark private centre.

I could hear their sharp and intrusive laughter being emitted in short, sharp bursts, through gaps in the crab-like shell of their huddled bodies as I walked along towards them. A hard, scaly body pointing my way, like something that might scuttle along a sea shore. No face. Just something vaguely threatening, and armoured against strangers. They didn't look up or notice me. They weren't really interested in me.

Then I saw a girl walking towards me in a thin, pink top. She was covering her breasts tightly with her arms folded neatly and snugly across her chest. But this defensive action of hers just managed to squeeze her large breasts upwards and nearly out the top of her tee shirt. I watched her walk slowly towards me, her large white breasts framed in that triangle of soft, smooth white arm and thin pink cotton, the soft white breasts dancing invitingly before my eyes. She smiled at me as she passed. I forgot to smile back, so she probably just saw another strained, hungry male expression, fixed in place. I smiled after she had passed, just a moment too late, and the smile just clung there that autumn night, before fluttering unsteadily away, like a dead leaf, its time already passed.

It was a dead sort of smile.

Behind me I could hear the lads say things to her. Compliments at first, softly spoken, seductive even, persuasive, but the compliments soon descended into crude obscenities, spoken and then shouted as she continued her journey. I looked back and the girl was walking faster, almost running away from them. I could see the strap of her bra jut out through the thin material, I could see her breasts from the back. The lads were gesticulating after her, wildly. All vigorous up and down, forward and back movements along long, distended poles. Long flag pole members. Three or four-foot long. I felt a little guilty because she had received no comfort from me and my draining of the detail from her body. At least those who were now making her uncomfortable were putting each other up to it. I had nobody to blame. But I comforted myself with the thought that my brother always said that I was too sensitive, particularly when it came to women.

'Treat them mean, keep them keen,' he liked to say. I had never tried. It wouldn't have felt right. It just wouldn't have felt right. For me.

Edelweiss was a little further along than I had anticipated. The garden was overgrown, long nettles now starting to falter after a long summer. I went back past the group of lads once more to fetch my car. I parked just outside my new home, taking great care with the hand brake because of the hill and made my way through the garden. I rang the bell, but it didn't work. I stood there in the silence for the street had gone quite quiet. I knocked several times and waited for an eternity for somebody to answer.

I could hear someone shuffling to the door and saying something. A woman with grey hair answered after a long pause. Her hair was brushed back carefully. Her thin face looked a little tanned in that light, but she still looked tired. Dark hollow rings filled in with layers of tan powder. She was wearing slippers. I caught myself looking down at the slippers, which I didn't like doing, because I couldn't work out how my eyes had got there. They were on a journey all of their own making, on an exploratory, defensive sort of excursion. I worried about what kind of face I might have been wearing.

She invited me in, watching me carefully, as if she was trying to work out exactly what kind of lodger I would be. She was smiling in the way that you do when you're greeting a complete stranger who you can't quite make up your mind about. It was a very asymmetric sort of smile. I notice these things. I think that I always have done, long before I became a psychologist. The house smelt very musty.

'I'm Frances … Frances Staunton. I'm pleased to meet you,' she said, after we were already in the house, which I thought was a little curious. I shook her hand, and thought of my friend John back in Cambridge and how he might react to contact with a stranger, and smiled to myself briefly again. She assumed that I was smiling at her.

She explained that she lived on the bottom floor of the house and that my bed-sit was at the very top. 'But I can hear everything that goes on in this little house of mine.' It sounded like a warning, or a test. It was as if she wanted to see my reaction. The house wasn't small for a start. She offered to help me with my bags, but I declined. It took quite a few journeys to get all of my stuff out of the car. She stood in the hall as I brushed past her with my heavy cases. When I had brought all of my belongings into the hall of the house, she led me into the living room that had a warm smell of stale food. An unpleasant odour. I caught myself breathing through my mouth for the time being, and periodically breathing back in through my nose as if to check that this smell was still there. It was. I was wondering how long it would take me to grow accustomed to this odour, so that I could no longer even smell it.

'Is there a young woman in your life?' she asked in a friendly sort of way, but I caught her drift anyway. 'Because if there is, I would like advance warning if, and when, she intends to stay over. Plenty of warning.' She smiled again, but more warily this time. I told her that there wasn't at the moment. I sounded a little nasal because I was trying not to breathe.

'No, I won't be having any female visitors,' I said to my new landlady, 'just at the present time.'

My landlady told me that her ankles were too painful to walk me upstairs, so she gestured in the direction of my room, and handed me the key. So I made my way upstairs with my first load with my suitcase in one hand, and two briefcases in the other, and with the rucksack on my back, to a room overlooking the street.

I noticed that on each floor there was different colour carpet, the one with brown swirls giving way to a narrow red-flecked carpet that stopped by the doors of rooms, as if it had not been invited in, but was requested to wait outside. I somehow hoped that the decor of the room itself would be better. The further I ascended in the house the worse the smell got, as if I was approaching a room with some decomposing food left in a cupboard. When I got to the landing on which my room was situated, I realized that the smell definitely came from the room beside mine.

It's odd entering a strange room for the first time, knowing that it's going to be your new home. Knowing that in the near future others will enter this room and perhaps see something of you in it. I opened the door carefully, and switched on the light. There was no lampshade, so the light was harsh in my judgement. I made a mental note to make some allowance for that. You must never jump to conclusions too quickly. All that back-tracking takes valuable cognitive time. You have to be careful.

My eyes, temporarily blinded by the raw light, moved sponta-neously and instinctively towards the fireplace. There was an elec-tric fire with a note on it which said that it didn't work, and a gas fire next to it. I noticed that there was a fire extinguisher to the side of the electric fire. Somebody cautious had lived here. There was a blue hearth rug in front of the electric fire, the fire that didn't work. I thought that it should have been in front of the gas fire, if the previous occupant was being logical.

There was a wooden desk to work at, with its top drawer hanging at a jaunty angle. Opposite there was a Creda Corvette water heater beside a sink and a bathroom cabinet with a silver fish motif that had a large protruding mouth and an elaborate tail fin. I couldn't work out if this was for decoration, or merely a joke, an ironic stab at the kinds of people who might find this sort of thing sufficiently decorative to display in a prominent position. I was trying to compute mentally an image of my pred-ecessor in that room, a man, for it was clearly a man, who was quite possibly more ironic but less – can I say – rational than myself.

There was a Polarfrost fridge in the corner. I thought that it sounded like a good make. I opened the fridge door and I could see rust in each of the bottom corners. Somebody had tried to brighten this part of the room with a McEwans Lager teddy bear fridge magnet. I didn't see this as ironic. Just sad.

The room had been tidied before I arrived. There was one poster rolled up beside the litter bin. I opened it up. It was the Eurythmics. I thought that I had left my student days behind me, but clearly not yet. I had been fortunate up to that point in terms of accommodation, but then again, this was the North. My brother had warned me in his letters about some of the accommodation, but it was more than made up for by the spirit and the humour of the people he said. I had a poster of the young Chatterton on my wall down in Cambridge, his hand outstretched, the poison taking effect. I thought that it might not be appropriate for here. It was a present from a friend who had never made it to Cambridge. I would never have bought such a thing.

I sat down hard on the bed, and it squeaked. I imagined the landlady downstairs listening intently to me, as if she had installed some great detection system to catch any wrongdoing in that dusty room. I moved up and down several times to see what would happen to the noise. The bed springs creaked in rhythm. I stopped moving and the creaking died away slowly, a lingering passing of noise and of sense. When the squeaking finally stopped, just for an instant, I felt quite alone. I thought of the girl in the pink top, and imagined myself as one of those lads shouting after her, telling her what I would like to do to her. I heard myself saying the words. Their words. Just to see what it felt like. One of the gang able to say just whatever I liked.

I glanced out the window, and I could see the gang of lads still there, laughing and smoking and joking away. It was as if they sensed me looking down at them. One of them looked straight up at the window of the room with the bare light bulb hanging from the ceiling. We made eye contact. I could feel the menace in it. I felt guilty as if I had been caught impersonating them for a cheap thrill. I broke eye contact immediately and pulled the orange curtains tight shut. I thought of their words as I stood there behind the closed curtains, with their long extended articulation, like words that they never wanted to have finished with. Words that they couldn't put down.

I noticed that the curtains matched the two cushions in the room. Someone had gone to that degree of trouble to blend the decor. I laughed even louder. But perhaps it was just naked relief.

I moved around the room getting my bearings. There was a little blood on the pillow, very old, almost black. I looked at it carefully, and tried to scrape it off, thinking about whether it had come from a nose bleed or something else, perhaps something more violent. Or from sex. You couldn't tell. It just lay there. There was no personal history written into it. It was a sign rather than a signifier.

I think that's the right way round. What I mean is that it told me something, but I didn't know what. Perhaps it was from somebody old before the house was divided into bedsits. Perhaps it was part of the final scene of the old and retired previous owner of the property, before the new landlady and the temporary students and the rooms full of beer mats and tatty posters and fridge magnets. Perhaps, it was therefore a signifier of evolution and change. Or on second thoughts maybe it was just a sign of violence and the lads on the corner and their crab-like and malevolent being, accomplished through their togetherness.

You really couldn't tell, and that troubled me a little.

# SIX

I left my bags unpacked and made my way back down the stairs. They creaked. She was sitting watching television with her bandaged ankle up on a stool. She asked me if I would like some tea. I glanced down at the bandages on her ankles, as if to say 'No, it was alright,' but she could see me looking. 'Oh, don't worry about them. I can still get about.' She pulled herself up slowly, with a considerable effort. Her face winced with pain. 'I've got ulcers on my ankles,' she said. I nodded cheerfully.

'You were a student recently, weren't you? What did you study then?' she asked from the kitchen.

'Psychology,' I said. 'Scientific psychology.' I stressed the word 'scientific'.

'Oh, I'll have to watch what I say then. Can you read me like a book?' she asked.

'Not really,' I said with a slight laugh in my voice, as if I was being overly modest, as if I really could.

'Where did you go to college?'

'Cambridge,' I answered.

'You must be able to then. Go on read my mind. Tell me what I'm thinking.'

She brought the tea in and sat back down on the settee. I sat there looking at her with her ulcerated ankle on a small vinyl stool in front of her. She obviously didn't get out much. She was glad of the company. That was probably why she had lodgers, for the company.

'Well, psychology is not an exact science,' I said, 'but it is a science nonetheless.'

'Lovely,' she said. 'I can see that it's going to be interesting having you here. I always mix psychology up with that other thing. What do you call it? Those men that people go to for a wee bit of help.'

'Psychiatry,' I suggested. 'And there are plenty of women too.' I meant that there were plenty of female psychiatrists, but she misunderstood me.

'Oh yes, there are plenty of women with problems,' she said. 'There are plenty of women in this town with terrible problems, what with all the unemployment in their men folk. They could do with a little bit of psychiatry. Anyway, you were going to read my mind. My life is a bit of an open book anyway. You can just tell me what you see.'

She leant back in the chair, and I could see her slip underneath her dress. There were photographs on the sideboard behind her, one photograph of a beautiful young woman of perhaps twenty and a handsome young man both dressed up and smiling for the camera. The glass was dirty, and you could imagine that late at night when the lodgers were tucked up in bed, she would reach for the comfort of that photograph. There was a snap of her and her husband in the summer in some sand dunes, she in a floral swim suit, and he in shorts that looked a little baggy on his skinny frame. They were older now. His hair was receding, she had put on weight, but both were smiling quite naturally.

I looked from the photograph to her sitting in front of me, hardly able to walk, waiting expectantly for the young man from Cambridge to interpret her tell-tale signs. Where would I start? With the tear stains, or the loneliness or how unfair life can be?

Suddenly, I could hear a key in the door. But the person was having trouble getting the door opened. I was pleased that we were going to be interrupted.

'Is that you, Robert?' she called out. 'It's only Robert who can't get the key in properly.'

A large man in his mid-thirties walked in, and eyed me up and down suspiciously. He didn't smile. He just nodded. He was bulky with reddish-coloured hair and a reddish beard flecked with premature grey. Untidy, sweaty, bad bodily odours. He carried three or four books. I couldn't see their titles, but it was serious reading. They had dull, dark green covers. He smelt of beer. His heavy bulk sat down opposite me. The tired old green settee gave out an audible sigh of exhausted air with his weight. He sat with his arms folded and watched me carefully.

'Alright, duck?' he said to me. I nodded and smiled at him, but he didn't smile back.

'This is your new neighbour', said the landlady.

'Oh', said Robert.

'He's a psychologist,' she said, 'from *Cambridge.*'

'Oh *Cambridge,*' said Robert, as he pushed his chair slightly back. 'Anything that he says is got to be worth hearing if he's from the home of the intellectual elite, the establishment, the ruling class.' He looked at me with a distinct prejudicial anger.

'I bet he hasn't been this far north before. I bet that it's a bit cold up here for him.' And he reached across and poured himself a cup of tea. I watched him stir the sugar into his tea slowly, and he looked my way again, warning me off with his expression. I could tell that he didn't even like how I looked, it was obvious that my fresh-faced boyish looks irritated him, as if here was a lad wet behind the ears who thought that he could teach him a thing or two.

'What do you do specifically then?' he asked in a way which told me that he had already made up his mind about the substantive nature of what I might say.

'Well, I work on nonverbal communication,' I said.

'Oh really. You know what they conclude from all that work,

don't you Frances? That we're all frigging baboons. Isn't that right? All baboons with our dominance hierarchies and our submission displays, with all those top dogs in the council up here walking into the room letting their ...' He hesitated slightly. 'Letting their big bollocks swing in front of them. Sorry about the language, Frances. But that's how they talk about us. Isn't that right? We're all naked frigging apes or living in the human frigging zoo? Not quite human anyway.'

He was staring straight at me. 'It's just more bloody propaganda from the establishment down Cambridge way. Isn't that right? Naked frigging apes. That ass-hole Desmond Morris was from Oxford wasn't he? We may be naked apes up here, but I bet down in Oxford they think that they're something different altogether.'

'That's not really right,' I said. I let the words come out slowly and in a sing-song way. I sounded very unsure of myself for some strange reason. He laughed and glanced at my landlady for support.

Like most students of nonverbal communication, I have to confess that I was for a time interested in the origins of human behaviour. I had studied the bared-teeth scream face which you see in lower primates and considered how this expression shown in fear and used in submission displays eventually evolved into our smile. I had studied young primates using an aggressive play gnaw accompanied by a kind of barking and considered how this became through the evolutionary millennia the human laugh.

Not unlike his, at that point in time.

I may have started with the most primitive processes between people, but I had built my picture of human beings up from there. Later I put human language back into the picture. That was the whole point of what I was doing. Making it all *human*.

But I couldn't explain that to him at this precise moment, sitting there with his legs wide apart, leaning back in the chair, like some big hairy ape waiting to be fed. I looked at him with that aggressive expression on his face, trying to knock me down with his crude verbal attacks and I thought of baboons throwing missiles at each other. I have to admit this. The image in my mind at that precise moment was of a large baboon with mangy grey-flecked fur wanting to savage me.

'Robert's up most nights until the small hours reading in that room of his,' said my landlady, as if oblivious to all these goings-on. 'He never goes to bed, you know. He's at it all night.'

'Oh that's nice,' I said. 'Do you not have to get up in the morning then?' I asked. 'He's studying', said the landlady interrupting.

'That's right, I'm a student', said Robert, 'even though I'm not formally registered anywhere.' He stressed the word 'formally', and looked at me directly for any response, indeed daring me to make any kind of negative judgment in my facial expression or elsewhere, no matter how fleeting or transient or unintentional.

'In official terms, I suppose, that I'm actually unemployed,' he continued. He made an aggressive and very obvious facial gesture this time. The privileges of power, I thought to myself. I have to conceal my emotions; he gets to display his openly. Indeed, so openly that they were trying to force me to empathize with him, but I was resisting, passive resistance that is.

'I'm one of Maggie Thatcher's special scholarship students, if you like,' he said. 'I read Hegel, Marx and Trotsky. That kind of basic stuff for starters. Thatcher very kindly has agreed to pay for my studies.'

'He's up in that room of his every night reading these big books,' said my landlady.

'But, *you* just study body language isn't that right?' he said, motioning my way. It wasn't really a question; it was more an accusation. 'The kind of stuff you get in Cosmopolitan and other women's magazines. No offence to women, Frances, but that's what he spends his time studying – how to flirt, how to impress your boss, how to kiss your boss's arse, how to get your leg over.'

'Well, it's not really body language,' I said, 'at least not in the normal sense.' It came out in that sing-song way again. 'And I'm not really interested in studying how to kiss anybody's arse, or even holding a seminar on this topic.' The joke went flat. 'Body language books are all just about people fixed in time and space, stationary, flirting without ever moving,' I said. 'People never move in these books and they never talk to each other. They just stand there not smiling, with their legs apart, their hands deep in their pockets, their groin pushed forward, saying "look at me, I'm a stud or whatever".'

I meant this to sound funny, but it didn't come out that way.

Robert was glowering in my direction. 'Stud or whatever', he repeated it twice, mimicking my somewhat bland accent and my even more desperate facial expression. And then he sat back in silence with his legs pointedly wide apart; he pushed his hands deep into his pockets for good measure. Luckily, he left his groin where it was.

'Body language is dynamic,' I said. 'It's constantly changing. Body language books say that posture signals attitude, but the problem is that people change posture all the time; they're always moving.'

'Yeah,' said Robert in a way that made it sound like a question. It meant 'so fucking what?'

'So,' I continued, 'if someone is sitting in a closed posture with their arms and legs folded one minute, which is meant to be negative, and then an open posture with their arms and legs open the next, which is meant, of course, to be very positive, does that mean that their attitude to you has changed?'

He now made an 'mmmm' sound, as if he was dealing with a great intellectual puzzle, but he was signalling that he was doing this mental computation in a highly ironic way.

'Or does it mean,' I said again continuing without commenting on his sarcasm, 'that they have started liking you?' I gestured towards him, as if to hand over the floor, but there was no response. He didn't even bother making any ironic sound. Not even a snort. 'Or did they really like you all along and it just took them a while to get going?' I relaxed back into my chair with that incisive point, that coup de grace. But there was no response.

I realized that this was not getting me anywhere. More silence. I looked back at Robert who I noticed had been sitting in exactly the same *very* closed bodily posture since I had started speaking.

'All communication is dynamic,' I said. My pitch had gone up. 'It changes all the time. Even the nonverbal communication of the great apes. Why should human communication be any less complex?' I added.

He stared back at me, without a single head shake, without a single nod or without … a single blink. Not one single blink as he listened to all of this. So this is what raw, naked aggression looks like, I thought to myself, it's completely blink-less.

'Who the fuck cares about any of this?' he eventually said. 'Sorry about my language, Frances, but have you ever heard such guff? He probably gets paid for spouting this stuff. There are millions unemployed up here, the great steel mills of Sheffield have all closed, the mines are all shutting down, the lives of the workers ruined, no prospects, their communities being dismantled and destroyed right in front of their eyes, and that's what he's studying.' He stared at me again. 'You should be ashamed of yourself.'

'And,' he added after a moment's reflection, 'he's actually getting paid for it. He's basically saying that we're no better than animals. I bet Thatcher loves hearing that. She probably gives you a bonus for coming out with all that stuff.'

He still wasn't blinking. 'What are you doing up here anyway? Are you planning to nip down to the Job Centre to study the naked apes being humiliated as they sign on? Are you planning to see how the workers deal with their frustrations with money and relationships and having to sit all day in the house looking at those four walls? Do you want to go and observe them nipping

into the supermarket in the middle of the afternoon so that they
don't bump into any of their old pals from the steelworks because
of the shame and the embarrassment of the whole thing? These
blokes were grafters, not layabouts. Thatcher has done that to
them, and sent you up here to say that they were just big, lazy
animals all along.'

My landlady looked away in her own embarrassment. I could
feel myself getting angry but I didn't want to show it. That's what
he wanted. I was here to follow my brother and show solidarity
with the working class. Why couldn't he see this?

But he wasn't finished with me yet. 'I suppose that if you
spend all your time studying body language, it means that you
don't have time to do any real psychology, like what really matters,
like people's hopes and dreams and aspirations for their kids, their
values, their *lives*.'

'Or *my* life,' he added after the slightest of pauses.

A long silence started to develop but this just acted as a spur
for me to say something more to make my point. I had to say
something. 'But you see,' I said, as if I was talking to some under-
grad, 'the basic problem is that body language is really interesting,
it's dynamic, especially when people are interacting. Take us, for
example, we are not really *interacting* in the proper sense at the
present time.'

'What?' he said laughing. 'What are you on about?'

'Well, in psychological terms, I mean we're not really *interacting*.'
I emphasized the word 'interacting'.

'Oh I think I get it,' said Robert, winking over at Frances. He
seemed much more relaxed now that he realized he was talking to
a complete and utter fool rather than a sinister instrument of the
state. 'We Northern baboons don't even know how to interact. Is
that what you're saying?'

'And where's all the actual talk in all of those body language
books?' I continued. I was starting to sound desperate. Tutorials
in Cambridge were never like this. 'The people in these books

never seem to talk. But in real life, body language has to work with talk. Somehow.'

I stressed the word 'somehow' with a pause before it, as if what I had just said was the most profound thing in the whole world, and I waited for a response. I wanted him to ask about the connections between the two channels of communication. I wanted a question about Chomsky and semiotics, and theories of linguistic competence and performance, about conversational constraints on psycholinguistic processes, about stuff that I knew, stuff that I was familiar with.

But he had a different focus of attention. 'Can I ask you one simple question?' I nodded. 'What do you know about any aspects of frigging real life?' he asked in a very aggressive sort of way without any attempt to modify or soften it. '*Any* aspects ... Go on take your time.'

'I know enough,' I replied without any pause on this final insult of his, as he now seemed to be implying that I could be defined by my slight failure to answer, by the micro-pauses in my speech. 'Enough,' I repeated. I realized immediately that I should-n't have responded so quickly. I was feeling emotional, hurt, and I let it show. I sounded almost tearful. I wasn't used to this sort of attack. At Cambridge we would attack the argument, not the person, at least not directly. Not like this.

Robert smiled. He looked smug. Contented. He had won this battle convincingly and he, and I, both knew it. The confronta-tional politics of Thatcher played out in that front room. Class war reduced to this, the micro-politics of derision in front of an audience of one, or perhaps three, because we were *all* spectators on my own humiliation.

There was an embarrassing silence. Robert then just yawned, and my landlady glanced at her watch. 'Well, it's past my bedtime,' she said with a slight fleeting facial expression which indicated that she had had enough of this discussion and of this humiliat-ing spectacle.

She pulled herself to her feet slowly and carefully, and using the arms of the chairs pulled herself towards a room out the back on the ground floor. Robert and I sat in silence until she had left the room completely.

'Have you graduated yet in Cosmo studies?' he asked eventually. 'Or are you still trying?' He gave a short sharp beery laugh. I didn't answer. He got up and switched the TV on. *News at Ten* was on. Mrs. Thatcher was being interviewed in the middle of a crowd. Dennis was standing just behind her looking slightly out of place.

'I hate that fucking woman,' he said as he got up and turned the sound down, just leaving her making great silent and therefore meaningless lip extensions in front of us. 'As if you couldn't have guessed.'

He continued to watch her as a whole, swearing beneath his breath. I, on the other hand, just watched her gestures float through the air, drawing complicated mental configurations in the air for us all to see. I was momentarily transfixed by the iconicity of these subconscious representations. I thought that I could detect some interesting features in them, some *meaningful* features. It was just my Cambridge background, I suppose, sometimes it can be quite useful. We waited until she had finished then Robert got up and switched the television off, without asking me whether I was watching it or not. Or whether I'd noticed anything interesting in her interview.

'How long have you been unemployed?' I asked. I wanted to sound concerned, but in reality I suppose I just wanted to put him in his place.

'About a year,' said Robert. 'Give or take a few months, but who's counting.'

'And what did you do before?' I enquired. I thought of Robert and his large lazy body sitting in the stores department out the back of some garage. I imagined him sitting skiving in oily clothes, waiting for a customer so that he could go and fetch an oil filter or something for the bottom half of a carburetor. I imagined him sitting there, reading *The Sun,* waiting for the end of the shift. Don't ask me where such negative images came from. I just don't like dark and dank garages or car stores. It's just prejudice really.

He looked at me long and hard. 'I was down the mine for ten years, like my father and brother before me. Now they've tried to throw me on the scrap heap. "Try" being the operative word here. I can't watch that old bitch any more. I'm going to bed to read. I'll see you around, cock, we'll talk again when you've got something useful to tell me.'

He left me sitting there staring at the brown swirl patterns on the carpet. I thought that they were a little like Rorschach blobs. But no matter how hard I tried at that precise moment I could see absolutely nothing in them.

# SEVEN

It was now late November. I was settling in to a routine. Lectures to prepare, students to see. They came for tutorials in large groups that filled my narrow, angular office and sat in a long line, shoulder to shoulder, opposite me, sometimes in two rows. A front row and a back row. A string of bright, open faces that looked straight at me and never at each other. I could hardly see the back row, but I knew that they were gazing at me in long parallel lines of regard, watching my every move.

The psychology department at the university was a contemporary building full of sharp corners on the outside. It looked almost pink with the autumnal sun glinting off it. It had a modern shape with narrow corridors and doors painted in bright, primary colours. Reds, blues, greens. It was a world away from the Victorian torpor of the academic department at Cambridge. The porter, who was called Stanley, sat behind a glass partition. He had a thin moustache and a stammer. He liked to tell me all about his life in the steel mills, before he was made redundant and ended up here.

'Here' is all he ever called it. Here. Not the university, not this great seat of learning. Just here. The place where he ended up. 'Better than the scrap heap, I suppose. I can keep an eye on you lot for a start.'

He resented the whole thing, the students, the staff, the flexible hours we all worked, the lack of real graft, and he would often display his contempt for other members of staff quite openly to me, and his contempt for me, no doubt, behind my back.

The students never made notes in tutorials, which surprised me. At Cambridge all of the students made notes in tutorials. It was as if the Sheffield students felt, or as if they knew, that I had nothing interesting to say, which perhaps was true. They could sense my nervousness, and I could see theirs. Sometimes one would wait behind to ask me to explain something. Sometimes they would try to find out details of my life. They were never subtle about it. 'Are you married then?' said one pretty little Indian girl with a Northern accent, after a first year tutorial. She sat in these tutorials and giggled in the back row and I had hardly noticed her before, except as a distracting presence. She never spoke in tutorials, not even when directly addressed. I thought that she was too shy, until she stayed behind that is. I had never noticed how pretty she was, close up, until that moment. She had obviously watched me though. 'Why do you ask?' I said. 'Oh, I was just wondering,' she replied. 'Just testing my psychological knowledge. I think that I'm the expert here,' and she laughed at her own joke, and I noticed the beautiful white teeth set in full, ripe lips. I smiled back at her in a way that felt gauche and clumsy and inelegant in front of her neat, perfectly formed presence. I could smell her sweet breath; I was that close. She had invaded my territory, rather than the other way around. And I was paying the price, drawing in the smells first from her mouth and then from her body, like a dog sniffing the wind.

She could sense it, of course, and she left my office with a teasing walk, teasing me all the way, leaving behind a faint smell of expensive perfume that lingered for most of the afternoon. Every time I came back to the room, I could smell her scent afresh, and I thought of her immediately. An almost perfect eidetic image of her walk. I don't know whether this was for me or not. I had never watched her leave before. As the students left my office, my eyes would gravitate towards the open books lying on my desk. It was my way of signalling that I had more important things on my mind than long drawn out farewells. It was my way of signalling that I could not look after them in that kind of way, as if they were just girls passing in the street, and I was just a boy. But I did that day. I knew that I shouldn't have looked at her like that. I felt slightly guilty, because it just wasn't very professional. I felt my brother grinning down at me. 'Treat them mean,' the voice in my head said. 'All those little crackers.'

I would work in the department until six or seven in the evening, and then walk home alone, sometimes passing the gang on my street starting to assemble for the night, like the nightshift at a factory, or a silt deposit in a river estuary. The buildup would continue slowly until they eventually blocked the pavement.

Sometimes they would shout things at me in loud, deep voices as I passed.

'Hey' … 'cunt' … 'fuck brain' … 'ass wipe.' Once, one of the younger ones shouted 'ass white' at me, but I was sure this was just a mistake, rather than something deeper or stranger. Deep, disguised voices that didn't naturally belong to their thin, reedy adolescent wind pipes. And when I challenged them about it, as I sometimes did, they would stand in front of me with sober, unwavering faces and deny that the sound had come from them. Or from anywhere near them.

'Did you hear a voice?' one would say. 'Oh no,' came his friend's reply. 'I'm sorry we didn't hear it. It must be the wind. They call Sheffield "the Windy City". Do you know that?' I told them that I didn't. 'I thought that Chicago was the Windy City,' I said. 'Oh no, it's Sheffield.'

And I would walk away and then they would laugh and the deep, resonant 'hey' would come again from nowhere. And then they would trump and guffaw in laughter at their on-the-spot humour and great originality.

'Windy City. Hrrrrrrmph.'

'Hey, cunt face. Catch this. Hrrrrrmph.'

I would lie on my bed sometimes and watch them. Sometimes they got lucky with girls who joined them to hang about outside my bedsit. The two groups, aligned like opposing teams on the pavement, would insult each other for a while and then the distances would start to be broken down. I would go back to my books, and when I looked back out half an hour later, the boys would be with the girls, all in pairs. It was all oddly predictable. It was no great conquest, the girls looked as greasy as the boys. And as desperate.

That night my landlady pushed a note under my door telling me that she had a niece called Linzi who liked to go to clubs and that if I was interested she could take me into town and show me around Sheffield. I felt my spirits rise again slightly, but I tried to keep them under control. I wrote a note back to her saying that I would love to meet up with Linzi and that she should drop me a line telling me the time and the place.

'I'm ready, willing and able for anything,' I wrote somewhat giddily.

# EIGHT

I got a note from Linzi to meet her in a club in town. 'Inside the club', it read. The note was written in thick pencil on lined paper, but paid scant regard to the constraints of the lines on the page. It was child-like writing, large letters, clumsy. 'Be there', it warned in thick capitals at the bottom 'Or be square'. There were five exclamation marks at the end.

I bumped into my landlady that night carrying some Ovaltine up the stairs for Robert. 'He's poorly,' she said, 'he's been over-working again.' Then she asked me if I had received Linzi's note.

'She's very nice,' she said. 'Very outgoing, and I told her that you were all alone up here. She's told all her friends about you and they encouraged her to ask you out. Well, we are living in the modern world now. Girls can do that sort of thing.'

It was wet on the Thursday that I was going to meet her, misty on the street, when I set off to get the bus into town. The street was empty, even the gang wasn't in its usual place. I carried an umbrella, and got a number 57 into the city centre. 'Tell me when we get to town please,' I said to the driver, a man with a thin face and a faint moustache who looked very gloomy.

'We're in town now, luv,' he replied.

'The centre of town, I mean,' I said.

'Oh,' he said. 'Okay, luv. You want the town centre? I've got you.'

I sat at the back and shook my umbrella. A couple looked round to see what I was doing, and then went back to staring out of the window with the rain running down it. I was the last to get off the bus, and the driver tipped his imaginary hat at me. 'Have a good one,' he said. He sounded wheezy. He was smoking, and blowing his smoke through the open side window.

I glanced back at him and he was looking sadly out at the empty wet streets. Then the bus shuddered off slowly. I walked up and down the same street a couple of times looking for identifiable signs, Linzi had drawn a map for me with almost no detail, and then I saw some girls, huddled in the doorway of a shoe shop, sheltering from the rain and smoking. One was adjusting her tights pulling them up through her skirt, and wiggling her big fat bottom in an effort to get them up. I waited for her to stop by hanging around outside the shop, without watching. Then I asked them for some directions.

They looked surprised when I approached them, and crowded round for a look at the stranger. It must have been my accent. I mentioned the name of the club. They all made 'ooooooh' sounds. 'Fancy,' one said. 'Fancy,' said another like an echo. I wasn't sure whether the first meant 'fancy that', or 'fancy club', and I had no idea what the second meant.

'Up there, luv,' said a third, 'up those steps. Leave him alone, girls. He's lovely.' I left them laughing uproariously in the doorway, waiting for the rain to stop, having a good time in a shop doorway of all places.

Of course, I had a mental image of what Linzi looked like, with a name like that how could you not? Here goes, I thought to myself. It was like jumping into the deep end.

I joined a slow-moving queue at the back. Girls in light summer dresses bobbed up and down in the late autumn rain for warmth, just in front of me. One girl with long shiny black hair asked me if she could have my umbrella.

I said, 'No, not really.'

'Okay then,' she replied. 'Stick it.' And her friends all laughed. One large wide hipped blonde girl was wearing a dress decorated with pink and green condoms that had been blown up and pinned to the shoulders. She had pictures cut from magazines of naked men pinned to both the front and the back of her dress. I wasn't sure why. A large black man with an enormous cock stared at me every time she turned her back.

Her hair was flattened by the rain. 'I think that I'm going to be sick,' she said.

'Not here for fuck's sake,' said the one with the shiny dark hair. 'Wait until you get inside. It's warmer in there if we have to hang about waiting for you to finish gypping.'

Every now and again the girl with the dark hair would pretend to go down on the naked man pinned low on her friend's belly. She waggled her long-speckled tongue, a tongue stained red and purple with dark Spanish wine in front of him and made 'num num', 'num num' sounds.

'I should be so lucky,' she said, when she eventually straightened herself up.

I could see that she was getting quite wet, so I told her and her plumpish friend that they could share my umbrella, if they wanted.

'Fuck off, creep,' she said, and turned her back on me. 'I don't think that they should let creeps in here,' she said to her coterie of friends. 'What do you think, girls?' They threw me short disgusted looks and occasionally made comments about my umbrella.

'I hope that fucking well chokes you,' said the fat girl who was still threatening to be sick.

Eventually, I got to the door. A small bouncer with close cropped receding hair, much smaller than me, stopped me. He was staring at my umbrella.

'What's that?' he said, pointing towards it with a sharp movement of his forehead, as if he was head-butting someone even smaller than himself.

'An umbrella,' I replied.

'Oh,' he said. 'That's alright then.' And he motioned me in, still with his head.

I entered the warmth of the club and started to shake the umbrella with a delicate and controlled wrist movement. 'It's a very wet umbrella,' I said to the same bouncer.

He left his spot to stand in front of me. He was looking up at me. 'Don't push your fucking luck, mate,' he replied. 'Alright? Pay here and fuck off.' And he pointed to a bored looking black girl with large heaving breasts in a leotard, her breasts resting on a counter. She took my money without saying anything and nodded me in.

I made my way through a long dark tunnel with fluorescent lights on the walls that were flashing intermittently. I hadn't been to a disco for a few years, and college discos weren't like this. I was hit with the dark and the loud music and a thick pulsating wall of people that started a few feet from the end of the tunnel. I tried to ask a doorman where the lower bar was. But he couldn't really hear what I was saying, until I repeated it several times so close to his ear that I could see a ragged and festering scab on his ear lobe. He had obviously been bitten. But by what or by whom?

I was starting to have doubts about this club. He pointed casually over the heads of the people with a finger that was bandaged, the bandage just big enough to cover a severe bite.

'I hope that you've got a big malevolent dog,' I said loudly, but he didn't hear me. And I set off slowly and carefully, apologizing every time I made contact with a hot almost moist body. I threaded gingerly through all the narrow gaps in the crowd, until I could see the bright rows of bottles before me and the bum cheeks of the waitresses.

There was only one girl at the bottom bar, and she wasn't alone. She was quite small and perched on a stool, drinking. She had a distinctive face. I could see that even from the side. Recognizably different. But I thought that I might be mistaken in that light with all those people crowded around, pushing and shoving. It was hard to see.

She was sitting on a stool, chatting to a very broad-backed bald bouncer, with a shiny head that reflected a bright white light from a spot light attached to the ceiling and some woman with a thin, lined tired face who was smoking. Sucking in the smoke through hollow cheeks. A normal person might have avoided this spot because of the cruelty of the white light, but he looked like he had chosen this spot deliberately.

This one harsh, white light in a world of pink and red hues which made the rings under his companion's eyes look darker, and made her look much older. But he wasn't bothered. I could see that.

This small group seemed to have an invisible bubble around them, the edges of the territory marked by the bouncer's expansive posture with his hand outstretched on a mirrored pillar, stealing extra feet. I noticed the hand. It was enormous. He was taking up space in this club where there wasn't any. They were all laughing. But the laugh never knocked him off guard. He was vigilant, watching everybody and everything. Every now and again, he would glance behind him. Watching his back. I don't think that I ever realized until that very moment, that this was more than just an expression.

They didn't notice me at first. Not even him. I was at the edge of the crowd, part of it. Anonymous faces that were sensible enough not to attempt to break the skin of that bubble. I wanted a better look at Linzi's face, without going forward. I strained forward for a better look. It was that which he noticed. That odd straining posture. In that sea of faces and shapes, he picked that out. He was that observant in this territory of his.

If I had been watching him professionally rather than as part of it all, I am sure that I would have been very impressed.

He seemed to laugh and he came over to me and without saying anything he took my arm and led me across the gap. His fingers pinched the skin under my arms. He wasn't dragging me over, but it was forceful enough. I wouldn't have liked to have attempted to resist. I wasn't sure whether he knew who I was or not. He was nipping me. It was like being a child again, caught for some misdemeanour, dragged along and hurt kind of accidentally on purpose. I didn't like it.

'Well here he is, Linzi,' he said. 'Your date for the evening. Your Prince Charming. What's your name again?' I told him, I was blushing.

'So here he is,' said the bouncer, 'the Cambridge graduate. Is that correct? You're not from Oxford or Eton, are you?'

'No,' I said. 'I've just come from Cambridge actually.' I was surprised to hear myself using the word 'actually'. It wasn't part of my working vocabulary. 'Not tonight, of course,' I said. 'I mean,' I began, 'I haven't come from Cambridge tonight.'

'Of course not,' said the bouncer, imitating me by blocking his nose with his finger and speaking in a slightly nasal voice. 'Not tonight,' he said in this nasal way. He removed his fingers, wiping the bottom of his nose as he did so, as if he was blowing his nose.

'A bit of a brain box, eh?' he said. 'Here's Karen, my girlfriend who's in the security business with me and here's Linzi.'

Linzi shook my hand slowly and held it for a moment. She had small, stubby hands. We all stood there smiling, not knowing what to say.

'I'm Lenny by the way,' said the bouncer. 'Most people call me Big Lenny, but you can call me Mr. Lenny, if you like, or sir.' And they all burst out laughing, especially Linzi who rocked back and forward on her chair. Then there was silence again.

Lenny, Karen and Linzi all stood looking at me expectantly. Linzi took a long slow sip of her drink. There should have been no silence because of the volume of the background music, but there was a deep well of silence.

'So this is the real Sheffield,' I said eventually. 'It's been hit hard by the recession, hasn't it?' There was no response. Not even a nod. 'Are you all fortunate enough to have jobs?' I asked. It sounded stupid before I had finished saying it, but there it was, out on the carpet in front of me. I couldn't hold it in. And they all burst out laughing again. Lenny's eyes shut tight in mock mirth. It wasn't a real laugh. I don't think that any of them were really laughing.

'Well I do three jobs at the moment,' said Lenny, 'door work, security work and debt collection, not counting working as Linzi's minder. That's unpaid though.' And they all laughed again.

'There's plenty of work up here if you're prepared to be a bit flexible. There's so much debt that there are a lot of jobs in the debt recovery business, and that's just for starters.'

'Oh,' I said.

'And there's plenty of door work,' he added. 'Even the pubs need somebody on the doors now. All the pubs are getting really violent so that generates even more work.'

'Really,' I said again.

'Is that all that you're going to say all night? "Really" and "oh". I thought that you were going to be a proper university man. A proper gob on legs. I thought that you were going to be a right big mouth, like a proper Cambridge type. But you're the fucking opposite. Are you the strong silent type, or something? You're not such a big man in here, are you? Like a fish out of fucking water. Is that the problem? Have you never been in a top-notch club before?'

And he gestured around the bar area at the waitresses in leotards working the tills and serving the drinks, and the men queuing at the bar, leering over the counter at them, commenting on their bum cheeks.

'These are just the ordinary punters down here,' said Lenny.

'There's a wine bar as well. But that's just for VIP's really. Linzi will be up there later. But because you're new we thought that you'd feel better down here with the ...'

'Ordinary folks,' said Karen. 'The more common type of

people,' said Linzi. 'The fucking riff raff,' said Lenny, all more or less simultaneously.

I looked around and I said that there was no problem. Lenny told Linzi that it was her round. He told her to go to the centre of the bar to get served. I was dreading her getting off that stool. I don't know why. Well I do know why. It was like I had been set up, but the joke would only really start when she got down onto the floor. I tried talking to her so that she would stay there for a few moments extra.

'Are you working at the moment?' I asked Linzi.

'No, not just at the moment,' she replied.

'I'm trying to sort her out,' said her friend Karen.

'Oh, that's good,' I said. I had delayed the inevitable for perhaps a few seconds. She had trouble getting off the stool. That added a few more seconds onto the wait. I could feel my eyes moving away onto the wall behind the bar. Out of the corner of my eye, I could see Lenny nudging his girlfriend.

'I hope that you're not narrow-minded,' he said, sensing my embarrassment.

Linzi descended from her high stool into another world. She was transformed immediately from a small person on a tall stool to a dwarf on the floor. Lenny bent down low and pinched her cheek. 'Ain't she lovely? I call her "Bridget the Midget",' he said. 'We'll have a dance later, Bridge.' He said it very loudly as if he was talking to a deaf person or a dog. She was beaming.

Lenny was watching my response. He said nothing to me. He and Karen chatted whilst Linzi was away at the bar. I stood there quite alone amongst the common people, leering at the waitresses, drunk, bumping into me on the way past. I stood there, buffeted this way and that. For some reason I wished that I was up in the VIP bar. I thought that at least it would be quieter up there. And darker.

Linzi came back with the drinks on a tray. I held them for her, as she climbed back onto the stool again. She was more or less level with me. 'I'm not really a midget,' said Linzi to me. 'I believe the correct word is "dwarf". I'm a twenty-one-year-old with a twenty-one-year-old's body, but I've just got short arms and short legs. A midget has a nine-year-old's body.'

'Oh, I'm pleased,' I said, and then apologized for saying it. 'Don't be embarrassed,' said the bouncer, who was sneering at me. 'And stop apologizing for fuck's sake. Tell him about your mum, Linzi.'

'Oh, my mum's a dwarf as well,' she continued. 'She had it more difficult than me - in those days it was really bad. I didn't even realize there was anything special about me until I was ten. I went for a hearing test at a school clinic with my mum and as we were leaving all these kids surrounded us. They were just junior school kids but they were the same size as us. I thought they'd surrounded us because they thought I was deaf. Then it all suddenly clicked.'

I noticed her gesture at that point. I honestly noticed her gesture. Her hands rose up from the bar counter to her head and her fingers fluttered in the air like an idea slowly coming into life, as if the whole thing took a while to sink in. There was no clicking movement in the gesture. There was no suddenness in the realization. I wanted to point this out, to change the subject perhaps. But I didn't really know how.

'Up until I was ten I could pass as a small ten-year-old,' said Linzi. 'I'd always regarded myself as just being a little bit short, nothing special. It's only from that time that people started reacting differently. All of a sudden, people were staring and laughing at me. It was even worse if me and my mum went out together. My father is normal size, but he never walks with us - he always makes some excuse when we have to go to town, as to why he has to go first. He can't be ashamed of my mum, mind, or he'd not have married her, I suppose.'

'No, he couldn't be ashamed of her,' I said. 'He wouldn't have married her if he was.'

'Do you want to bet?' said Lenny, looking carefully at me.

'Some men can be right cunts,' said his girlfriend, Karen. 'I should know.'

Linzi took a gulp of her drink. 'But the big thing in my life is the CB circuit,' she said. 'Have you ever been on the circuit?'

'No,' I answered.

'Well, I have,' she said enthusiastically, 'and it's fantastic. Through the circuit I get to meet quite a few people and I met this guy who owned a removals firm. He said he needed someone to work in the office to take bookings by phone and talk to men in the vans over the CB. He said, "You're right experienced with CB's, you could do it." I was over the moon - my first job. I told my mum and she was so proud. I signed off the dole on Friday and went to see him on the Saturday.'

'That's really excellent,' I said.

'Well not really,' she replied, 'because he just burst out laughing when he saw me. It was just a joke, but I was so embarrassed. I had to go and tell my mum and my friends that I'd been set up. He thought the whole thing was hilarious - a dwarf working in his office. But it wasn't so funny from my point of view - the dole stopped my money for six weeks because they thought I'd been messing them about.'

Lenny was laughing openly now. It was my discomfort that he seemed to find funniest. 'Look at the face on that,' he said, pointing at me. 'Worth the fucking entrance fee that.'

'It was my friend who persuaded me to go to night-clubs to get me out of the house,' said Linzi. 'I know lots of midgets who never leave the house at night. I used to go on my own. My mum was really worried - she'd heard that in Australia they have competitions to see who can throw the midget the furthest. She'd seen it on TV. She was afraid that they'd start throwing me onto the stage in the night-club. I only met Lenny because there was this guy bothering me. Some blokes, when they're pissed at the end of the night, think that if they haven't pulled they might as well chat up a dwarf. I couldn't get rid of this bloke - he followed me to the taxi. Lenny had to follow him outside and sort him.'

Lenny pulled a chair out for me. I had no choice. I took a seat beside her.

Lenny said that he had to do his rounds. He left us together. A man and a woman in a night-club with the smoochies coming on.

'I like going out to night-clubs with Karen and there's always the possibility that I might meet someone,' said Linzi, sucking through her straw. She looked at me as if to test my reaction. I looked away immediately.

Another bouncer came up. 'Pulled again, Linzi, eh?' he said, touching her hand. 'She never fails that girl, you know. I don't know what her secret is.'

'It's just my great personality,' said Linzi. 'Don't you agree? Everybody tells me that I've got a super personality.'

'Oh yes, you're very easy to talk to,' I said.

'And I'm a bit tipsy tonight with all this brandy and Babycham. It's gone to my head. I hope that you're not going to take advantage of me.'

I could feel myself growing bright red, but I was hoping that it would be invisible in the red glow of the club. I thought of my brother and his letters about life in the North. I felt that I could hear him laughing.

I don't know why I thought of that image at that very moment. But I did. I was sure that if it had been brighter in there, everyone could have witnessed my look of pain.

'Time to leave ladies and gentlemen, please.' The small bouncer who had asked me about my umbrella was doing his rounds. 'Have you no beds to go to?' he asked and then winked at me. I didn't like the ambiguity of the wink. I looked blank. 'Nothing to be ashamed of,' he whispered in my ear, bending low to say it.

'Will you walk me to the taxi, please?' asked Linzi. 'I don't want to get bothered by all the guys who haven't managed to pull. They're always making comments to me about how they'd like to have a dwarf at the end of the night, if they can't get anything better, just to see what it's like.'

I said that I would and I walked with my eyes straight ahead so that I made eye contact with nobody. I could see Lenny coming to the door to watch us leave.

'Goodnight, sir. Goodnight, madam,' he said. He was laughing with another bouncer. I heard him saying something more. I couldn't really make it out.

Something about one nil to the Sheffield lads. Something about Cambridge snobs getting what was coming to them. Something about a bloody good lesson about psychology to plonkers who thought that they knew it all. Something bitter and unpleasant like that.

The Asian taxi driver looked at me with some distaste as Linzi climbed into the back of the cab. 'Will I be seeing you again?' she asked.

'Of course,' I said.

'Do you want to write your work number on the back of my hand then?' she said. 'We could come here again, or go to an *even* more up-market club and go to their VIP bar. I could introduce you to some of the really big hitters in this town.'

She tried to bend forward for a kiss. Her legs were off the floor of the taxi. She had to move along the seat using just her arms. I saw the taxi driver looking at me. He said something in very poor English. I think that it was hurry up, but I couldn't be sure. I put my hand through the window and shook her hand forcefully.

'I've just arrived here from Cambridge,' I said to the taxi driver. I'm a psychologist.' 'Oh,' he said. 'Cambridge. Very, very nice.'

I hoped that he would think that this was a professional encounter of some sort - helping the less fortunate - that sort of thing, because I was starting to realize that there are some less fortunate than others. The taxi driver's pitying look told me that. It was directed straight at me. I set off to walk in the rain all the way back to my digs.

# NINE

I liked to keep my room in the department quite dark late in the day, after the students had gone, in my first few months there, so that my focus was just what was on those bright figures in front of me. In the distance I could see some high-rise flats, now housing students, and at four o'clock in the afternoon the lights would go on in the flats and I could see lives being lived. In miniature.

But you could see almost nothing of any interest happening in those bare rooms in long afternoons gone grey with rain. Compared to this light in front of me. The brightness from the screen sometimes dazzled me.

I liked a large, magnified image of the people I was studying, so that even the smallest movement would be sharp and discriminable. A bright image full of contrast and shape. Hard edges. I was becoming very good at detecting even the smallest of tremors, in the way that you do with hundreds of hours of practice.

He was sitting there just in front of me. Quite still to begin with. Another student. They were all students. This one wore jeans and a striped shirt under a black denim jacket. The image was black and white. The shirt might have been blue and white perhaps, but that's just a guess. He wore glasses. I don't remember his name either. He wrote it down for me. It was hard to pronounce; I do remember that. I just called him 'glasses with foot out front' for reference purposes. That was the image I had of him on my bright screen. Glasses with black rims hiding the eyes, and a big black boot that liked to move across my screen as he talked. I could see his laces flicker as he moved.

I just used that title for personal reference purposes though. He was officially subject eleven. 'Glasses with foot out front' sounded to me like an impressionist painting. Blue bowl with olives, that kind of thing. I liked that sort of title for my video recordings. The art of conversation. That was what I was analyzing really. There is a lot of important detail in painting that most ordinary people miss.

He didn't look that comfortable.

The student on the screen was starting to move. His leg was pulled across his body, like a fragile, trembling barrier between him and me. His left foot was magnified in the foreground, with that gigantic flickering lace. His boot wasn't tied properly. The foot looked huge. With my hidden camera in the experimental room I could see the sole of his shoe.

A glimpse of his very sole. I thought of that joke one night. I would have liked to have told it to my brother. His head was tilted back at an angle looking up at the cartoon story that I had projected onto the wall for him. He had to tell me a story about what was happening in that cartoon. I used cartoon worlds as my focus. They were simple and engaging and not like the real world with its multiple embedded meanings and devious complicity. Cartoons were straightforward.

He looked very co-operative, submissive even. One hand was on his knee; the other hand was on the arm of his chair.

He was telling me a story about a cartoon character called Ivy the Terrible. It was from the Beano. Ivy had a single tooth. That was her trade mark. One tooth in her whole head and pig tails with two round, pink bobbles holding them in place, pink dungarees and a yellow sweater under the dungarees. Blue and white shoes. A female Dennis the Menace sort of character. 'Yahoo,' she liked to say when she was happy. 'Yahoo.'

I had started to say the word myself. I would say it sometimes on the way home. It just popped into my head, and I would say it, until I saw the gang of lads who never left that spot outside my digs. They knew where my room was and sometimes they would throw stones up against it, rattling the window. I watched one of them with a stick flicking a dog turd up against the glass. It clung there for many minutes before dropping languidly to the pavement. I had started leaving my curtains shut during the day, but that seemed to provoke them as well. They would call out, as if I was hiding behind the curtains.

I sometimes think that I preferred life in my office, dark with the screen bright in front of me. It was Ivy's nursery party. It was a simple enough story in that strange world of cartoons where infants can do whatever they feel like. Ivy was going on the rampage again. Ivy saw the DJ unpacking his equipment, so she locked him in the boot of his car, so that she could do his job for him. She played the music too loud, and put extra strong washing up liquid in the bubble machine, until you couldn't see any of the other children. Then she made the children form a long crocodile and they all congaed out onto the street. While they were out there she started to eat the party grub, beginning with a huge triangular sandwich. The kind of sandwich you only ever see in cartoons.

She was chomping on it. 'Chomp, chomp, chomp,' said the caption. She had locked herself in the room with the party food so that she would not be disturbed. 'Clunk' went the lock.

She got her come-uppance in the end though because bubbles had got into the sandwich. Somehow. The last picture was of Ivy with all these bubbles coming out of her mouth, and a look of disgust on her face. Her eyes shadowed with sickness.

There always seems to be some distress at the end of these stories. I had noticed that from using them in my experiments.

That seems to be the point of cartoons.

Somebody always gets it in the end. In this story, Ivy got her come-uppance; over the page Billy Whizz caused distress to his whole family. His family was hanging from a table suspended in the air, with fear written all over their small faces. They had tried to get away from him. That was why they had to suffer.

The student in the striped shirt and others like him told me the story of what was happening in these cartoons and I video-recorded them with a hidden camera. I could have analyzed their posture and their uncomfortable positions, but that wasn't what I was interested in. It was their hand movements. And what these hand movements might tell us.

I sat there watching 'glasses with foot out front' get to the point in the story where Ivy was starting to eat the food, with her classmates locked outside. He said, 'she's eating the food'.

But then I watched perhaps a hundred times what he did with his hands whilst he said this. This was the crucial bit. The incredible detail in all of this. His left hand was resting on his left knee, which was positioned between stomach and chest level. The palm of his left hand was oriented downwards; his fingers were slightly apart. He rotated his hand so that the palm now oriented towards his body. At the same time his hand started to move quickly upwards towards his mouth. This hand rose to shoulder level; his fingers closed together until they touched. Then his hand rapidly moved downwards, the fingers opening slightly. The hand then returned to its original equilibrium position. It was now temporarily at rest.

This all happened in seven hundred milliseconds. Seven hundred milliseconds crammed with sense and meaning.

Of course, to the untrained eye it might look like an inconsequential shrug. A random shift of the hands. Perhaps an index of how uncomfortable he really was in front of me doing something that he did not really understand. Telling a cartoon story to a Cambridge-educated psychologist.

I had deceived him, of course. I simply told him that I was recording what he was saying with a tape recorder, and that he should tell the story as best he could. What he didn't know was that there was a video camera pointed straight at him, capturing all of this densely packed information.

But this was no shrug. There was nothing inconsequential in any of this. I discovered that by playing bits of this tape to people, those who saw the gesture accompanying 'she's eating the food' knew that Ivy was eating something sandwich shaped. They knew that the sandwich was big. They knew that the sandwich was being drawn up to the character's mouth. Without the gesture there, they sometimes thought that the food was on the table in front of her, and that Ivy was using a knife and fork to eat it.

These little inconsequential flicks of the hand did all that. In other words, body language isn't body language at all. Not in the sense that everybody talks about it. It's not all about fancying him or her, or about emotion or about anxiety or lies or pain, it's about the world out there. The real world. Some magnificently intricate conceptualizer in the human mind activates both speech and hand movements simultaneously. Body language isn't separate from speech the way that everybody thinks. They're part of the same system. They're one and the same.

I desperately wanted to tell my brother all about my research. The mind and the body in action together, negotiating meaning in tandem, in the great society of human minds. Beyond the primates with their teeth bared, beyond books about how to read the signs and signals of hot women in everyday life, who had their tongues cut out and discarded somewhere along the way.

That night my mother rang. I tried to talk to her about my work but she didn't want to listen to me; she just said that people like me do things and say things that ordinary people like her, and like my brother, just can't understand. Then she started sobbing about how alone she was in this world.

I had trouble sleeping that night. It was a mixture of excitement tinged with anxiety, I suppose. Excitement with my work, and the rest a mild and barely articulated anxiety.

Linzi had rung me at the house that day several times, but I hadn't returned her call. I was worrying about her calling round. I didn't want to be rude.

Eventually, I fell asleep that night and disturbed dreams came my way. Linzi and I were alone in some flat at three in the morning. I don't know how I knew the time, but I remember that it was about three o'clock. Back from a club, that's it, but the club wasn't part of the dream. But something must have happened there. At the club, that is, because I was with her. Nothing to do with body language, I was just with her, I knew that. Then I was sitting on the edge of a strange bed, uncomfortable and embarrassed. I didn't know where she was and then I realized that she was on her knees in front of me, starting to unfasten my trousers, as if she had crept up on me.

Then I heard her try to speak, but I could still detect those Northern vowels. 'They always try to pull dwarf at the end of the night,' she was saying. It was a long 'ah' sound. She was chomping on me like Ivy the Terrible. I was laughing in my sleep. My world of cartoons was with me in my dreams. 'You all go for fucking dwaaarf, when your mates aren't watching.'

Then in my dream I heard a voice from behind. It made me jump. A voice from the shadows. A disembodied sort of voice. It didn't belong in this cartoon world.

'Who wants to fuck dwarf then?' it said. There was no definite or indefinite article. It was always 'dwaaarf', never 'the dwarf' or 'a dwarf'. It was Lenny's voice. 'Line up, line up.' It was insidious, chummy, he sounded like a circus master, or a pimp. 'Fucking marvelous,' he whispered in my ear, and I looked round at him and his hands parting slowly to a distance of about nine inches to represent the legs opening.

But only so far apart. I laughed in a distracted sort of way now, a dreamy sort of way, thinking about those short legs wide open.

Then the laughter became louder until it woke me up. I was sweating profusely from anxiety. My belly was wet and it wasn't just sweat. I sat in the dark, wiping the wet slowly off my belly. I felt uncomfortable, disturbed by it all, distressed.

But eventually I managed to work out that this dream was really about my work. It was obvious really.

It was about how speech and gesture work together across modality to form a single representation of the world. That was it.

It was Lenny's gesture, his hands opening up simultaneously with what he was saying I needed both his speech and his gesture to understand what he was offering me.

That was what this dream was all about. It was just my academic work invading my unconscious. That was its latent message, as Freud would have said, even though I should say that I am no great fan of Freud. The particular topic was incidental. Linzi was just a detail, an irrelevance. So too was Lenny, whispering in my ear, playing the pimp, goading me.

It just shows you the danger of allowing your work to take over your life. Even for a psychologist.

That, at least, was what I had managed to convince myself of, by the time the light eventually filtered through my curtains, illuminating my sweat soaked bed with the damp sheets pulled to the centre of the stained mattress.

# TEN

I was starting to enjoy my life at the university more and more. My mother said that it would take a few months for me to settle in, and she was right. For once. My research work was taking off. I had invites to present seminars in Cardiff and Durham on my work on speech and gesture, and a very complimentary letter about my research from the leading international researcher in the field from Chicago. It was signed 'David'. 'Keep up the good work,' he wrote.

I pinned it on my wall, and circled the sentence with a red pen, as if strangers who came into the room might recognize immediately who David was. And know something about me.

My professor was pleased with my progress. I could sense that every time we talked. He was now talking about research grants and perhaps even a centre for human communication research right here in Sheffield. He was even talking about interest in the applied possibilities of our research, including forensic possibilities. This excited me.

It was always 'our research' now. I knew what that meant. I had been warned about that sort of thing back in Cambridge.

'A new angle on human interaction,' my professor had said. 'And why not? A new centre of excellence. In Sheffield. And why not? It could be very profitable … academically, of course.' My brother would have laughed at his little rhetorical flourishes and his metaphors and his images. We were all entrepreneurs now, it seems, all looking for an angle on something. All looking for something to sell. That was what Mrs. Thatcher had achieved. We were all hoping to become Blake Carrington from Dynasty, even the academics.

I was starting to enjoy the pattern of life in the university, the energy of the students in the darkening days of winter as we crowded into the one common room for staff and students. A smoke-filled den of intrigue and nebulous excitement. I was enjoying the laughter and the smiles as I passed. The attention I got. That was what it was really. The attention. No doubt Freud could explain that the way he explained everything else.

Vaguely.

I craved a mother's attention as a child. Unrequited attention. Attention that I never got. So I was overcompensating now. What did Freud call it? A 'reaction formation'? Is that the term? But a reaction to what? And what sort of *formation* is that?

What is attention after all? Just sustained looks. Just eye gaze. The stuff I've examined in the past. The stuff that I've mathematically modelled. Just micro-patterns of eye behaviour probably not half as interesting or as meaningful as those gestures that I keep on my screen. Not even a quarter as interesting as those.

I loved the attention from faces that I didn't necessarily recognize but faces that recognized me. I was getting used to all that attention. Bright, open faces hanging on my every word in tutorials and lectures. Even the gossip about me. I could hear my name being mentioned. I didn't know what they were saying, but that was unimportant. They were talking about me. Not my brother. Not the boy with the maternally cultured eye brows nor the socialist at Orgreave, inspiring the workers with his rhetoric. Nor the man who nearly climbed Everest. But me.

I felt important and wanted. I felt at home perhaps for the first time ever, where I belonged, at the centre of converging looks.

Nila would come to see me after tutorials and look up at me

through that long dark fringe of hers. Of course, she was out of bounds for me, but if I am being truthful I relished all the attention from her. And the letters.

Oh, yes the letters. Poems, letters in a smooth flowing writing style that covered four or five pages. I was, she swore in her letters, her very first love and she said that she knew one day perhaps when she graduated that we would be together. There was an innocence about the letters. I enjoyed talking to her and that fresh, innocent smell when she sat even closer. But neither of us ever touched. Not even accidentally.

My mother would ring me in the middle of the afternoon, after perhaps the first drink of the day. But I was becoming more sympathetic. I wanted to listen. And when she talked about loss and how nobody in the world feels loss like a mother, I still listened. I really tried. But I still couldn't bring myself to talk about my loss and my suffering. How could I? She would have said that I had everything going for me. All that privilege, all that education. All those advantages that my brother or her or my father, the man who was rarely mentioned these days, never had.

So I kept it to myself. I personally think that talking is over-rated anyway. It's all Freud's fault. I blame him.

I was happy in the confines of the university, like Lenny was happy in that club of his. It was an ivory tower of sorts, I suppose. If his club was an ivory tower. But late one spring day things were to change. There was a knock on my door whilst I was in the middle of a tutorial and in she walked. She didn't wait for me to answer, she just walked straight in. That, I suppose, might have been some kind of omen.

She was wearing a pink sweater, and had a newspaper cutting hanging limply in her hand. I recognized the photograph. It was me in the middle of a gesture. It wasn't a real gesture, of course. It was an exaggerated one. The local paper had done an article on me entitled 'Matt's Mission'. They had failed to understand the points I was making about gesture. 'Magnus Pyke does it, David

Bellamy does it, now a psychologist in Sheffield is studying it,' it read. But those theatrical gestures performed for the camera were not what I was interested in. I was interested in the mind trickling out through the hands and the fingers, something different altogether. I had torn the article up.

But that was what I noticed first. Not the cutting, not the photograph, but the bright pink sweater. The tight pink sweater and white leggings and high white stilettos. All of the students in their blacks and their dark browns stared at this stranger in their midst. This stranger with blond curly hair tumbling over her shoulders.

'Can I help you?' I asked, thinking that she might be lost, and somehow ended up in a psychology department of all places by mistake. 'Are you Matt?' she asked. 'Matt Jones?' She had a high girlie voice. I nodded. 'That's me.' 'Are you Phil's brother?'

'Yes,' I said. I felt myself getting excited. Nobody called him Phil, except people who knew him very well. He only allowed those very close to him to call him that.

'I'm Adele. I'm his ...' she corrected herself. 'I was his girlfriend.' And then she burst out crying, her face folding in on itself, in grief, like a paper flower crumpled in someone's hand.

The students sat there, not saying anything, until I asked them to leave. It was as if they didn't have enough sense to be able to tell when it was their time to go. They all moped out, except Nila, who clearly didn't want to leave me in the same room as that heaving, sobbing, blonde girl in front of me.

'Can we have an essay topic for next week?' she asked, as this girl stood in the corner of the room crying into a wet tissue.

'I'm sorry, I can't talk to you now,' I said to Nila. 'Can you come back tomorrow?' And I made a gesturing movement towards the far stairs. She slammed the door as she departed, making fragments of chipped paint fly off towards me.

I sat down quietly behind my desk and told Adele to take a seat. She asked for a hanky. She blew her nose loudly several times.

'I saw your picture in the paper,' she said, passing me the wet hanky. 'I knew immediately that you were his brother. It wasn't just the name; it was the eyes that told me.'

'Oh,' I replied.

'I'm an expert on eyes,' she said. 'They say that they're the windows on the soul.'

I made a faint laughing sound and heard myself saying 'I suppose they are,' although, of course, I don't believe in such poetic tosh.

'Phil talked about you all the time,' she said. 'But I didn't know that you were a psychologist. I thought that you were younger for some reason.' I looked at her large grey eyes, still welled with tears, and wondered how mean my brother had been with her.

'And then when I read the article and found out that you worked on body language too,' she continued, 'I couldn't believe it. Your mother must be very proud.'

'She is,' I said. 'She is.' I was wondering why she had said 'too', but I didn't like to comment on this. I assumed that she was referring to herself.

'I only found out about his death in a newspaper,' she said. 'There was a picture of him with that smile of his. He was so tanned and so well.' She sobbed again. I passed her the wet hanky back, and then apologized. 'Did he ever talk about me?' she asked.

'It's so long ago,' I replied. 'It was a difficult time.'

Her name was vaguely familiar. I had gone through my brother's clothes after his death, removing all of the personal things before they were sent to Oxfam. My mother wanted me to keep his clothes and wear them. But that would have just been for *her* benefit. I had come across the name Adele written on the inside of a packet of matches. A name printed in smudged lipstick with a telephone number beside it. It was in a coat pocket, along with a string of faceless Joannes, Clares and Michelles, their names and numbers jotted down in pink or burgundy or fuchsia lipstick or thick blue eye-liner on scraps of jagged beer mat, ripped apart in that frantic egotistical haste so late at night. All the names written in a heavy, intoxicated sort of hand, sometimes with a big bold 'X' beside them. Or an 'X X X.' They lay there in his coat, trophies of a sort, I suppose.

'I have come across your name,' I answered more or less truthfully.

'I'm sorry that I barged in on you like this,' her eyes were lighting up. Almost sparkling, the heavy drops of salty tears in the well of the eye, and in great round dollops at the side, reflected back the light.

'Was that the teacher's pet then?' she asked, gesturing outwards towards the door. 'That little dark haired thing who wouldn't leave.' She made the same gesture again. 'Sort of,' I said.

'She looked very pretty,' she said, 'but you couldn't really tell because of the length of that fringe. Tell her from me that she should have that cut.'

'Are you a hairdresser then?' I asked with a slight smiley voice.

'Not really,' she said. 'I used to be a nurse, but I'm a sort of beautician, now. Not a sort of beautician, I mean a real beautician, sunbeds, nails, facials, body waxing, that sort of thing. Bikini waxes. That's why I'm so brown, you see,' she said, and she lifted up her tight pink jumper so high that I could see more flesh.

'My tummy always goes brownest,' she said. 'I'm very proud of my tummy.' And she held the jumper up for an eternity in front of me as my eyes took in every detail of her beautiful brown skin covered in goose bumps. 'I must be cold,' she said. 'I must need warming up.' And she rubbed her sides and let the thin cashmere material slide back down slowly.

I passed her another loose hanky from my drawer without really looking. I noticed, as I handed it to her, that it had some felt tip red ink on it. Probably from the ink that I had used to highlight David's letter. The department always used the non-permanent variety. I don't know why. The ink got everywhere. Now, it was on the end of her nose. I couldn't let her leave like that. I reached across to rub it off gently. I'm sure that I said 'Excuse me.' But she couldn't have heard.

As I started to rise slowly and reached across my desk to wipe the ink off, she stood up and reached forward and started to hug me, pulling me in closer to her, until only my toes were on the ground. We stayed in that odd position, hugging with a desk between us for perhaps two or three minutes, without saying a word. She smelt wonderful.

I know that Nila was watching from the street below. I glimpsed her as my head turned to get into position. She was standing there, her shoulders hunched and knotted. I think that I saw her facial expression, but I can't be sure. But there was nothing I could do. I was stuck. It was as simple as that. I was stuck in the arms of my brother's ex-girlfriend. I closed my eyes and breathed in deeply. A glorious fragrance of warmth. She was hugging me tighter until at that angle across that desk, my feet were barely touching the floor. And I was enjoying every precious second of it.

# ELEVEN

I arranged to meet Adele that night, and she came in a taxi to pick me up at my bedsit. We drove across town, without saying that much but the silence felt comfortable. Every time that I glanced at her she appeared to be smiling back at me.

When we stopped, she paid the taxi driver, holding my hand back to do so. I felt her long manicured nails bite into me accidentally to stop me getting my wallet out of my jacket. It felt good. One nail left a small crescent shaped mark on my finger. I rubbed it, as I got out of the taxi. I didn't mean to. It wasn't even a scratch.

'Baby,' she said, and she took my hand and rubbed it gently. I liked how she said this. She could tell. Don't ask me how. She laughed and then pouted her lips and said it slowly in my face. 'Baby. Is that better? Baaaaaby.' Each time different. Each time better.

We had stopped outside a casino with bright gold lettering down the side. I had never been to a casino before. There was a queue to get in, but she took me by the hand and led me up the side of the narrow line, and straight in. I could see everyone watching us. A couple of faceless men made some comments to her. Sexual comments under their breath. To each other. Never daring to direct them even towards her. She looked straight ahead.

'Ignore them,' she said. She was laughing. 'You know what

they say. Ignore them, and they'll go away.'

The doormen in their black ties all greeted her warmly. 'Good evening, madam,' they said. 'Good evening, young sir,' they said to me.

She signed me in. She asked me my address and then said it didn't matter. 'I'll put mine.' I recognized the area in which she lived. It was pricey. Very west side of town. We went down some steps to a restaurant with candles on the table and brown-black tinted glass overlooking the gaming area. I asked her if those playing roulette and blackjack could see us. I was sure that one handsome, young male croupier, slightly foreign looking, Moroccan perhaps, showed some recognition of her. He had smiled our way, but she didn't smile back. 'We're just dark shapes to them,' she said.

It reminded me a little of my laboratory set up with my one-way mirrors behind which I kept my video-recorder. I mentioned this to her. 'And my place too,' she said excitedly, squeezing my hand. Then she corrected herself. 'Not the beauticians … I work on the reception in a club at night. They have glass like that there too.' I told her that I thought that she must keep herself very busy.

'I do,' she said. 'It's the only way to make ends meet around here in this dead end town.' There was a sadness about how she said the word 'dead', but perhaps 'sadness' is too strong a word, more a world weariness.

The waiter came quickly, and smiled at her. It was a genuine smile. I could tell that. Not a cursory professional flick of a smile. He glanced at me more warily, as if he was trying to work out whether he had ever seen me before. I smiled at him, but he just glanced at his pad in reply. She ordered for me without even looking at the menu. 'Is that okay?' she asked.

'Fine,' I said. The waiter looked down at me as if I was some punter who knew little about fine food or fine wine. I thought that she liked being in charge.

She told me about her life before meeting Phil, and explained that she had worked as a nurse on a spinal injury ward for three years, but couldn't take it any longer. 'The shifts, the pay, being knackered all the time,' she said. 'The same men in over and over again. As soon as their family get fed up looking after them, they'd be back in for us to take over. You got attached to them over the years.'

'I can imagine,' I said. I could see her eyes going back to that time. They were almost wistful.

'It was a happy time. But it does your back in eventually,' she said. 'I sound like an old woman.' She sipped her white wine. 'All that turning them for their bed sores. And some of the cases are so tragic. We had one guy in who jumped out of a window. He wanted to end it all. He had been laid off from work. He was a steel worker. But he didn't even do that right. He broke his neck. He kept his suicide note on his locker. "Put it down to unemployment", he had written. He would stare at this for hours. It used to make him cry at nights, and then we'd have to comfort him.'

'He must have had his guardian angel looking after him that night,' I said, thinking of my brother.

'Or not', Adele replied. 'He hated being alive and being a quad.' I must have looked puzzled. 'A quadriplegic,' she said laughing slightly. 'That's what we called them. They didn't really mind,' she added after she noticed that I had stopped smiling. 'You have to call them something.' I didn't say anything.

'That's what they called themselves after they'd been in with us for a while,' she added. 'You had to laugh about it. It was the only way any of us survived.'

I could see what my brother saw in her. She was beautiful with a face that lit up when she talked. Eyes that picked up the light and guided you in from the dark. And she had a wonderfully voluptuous body. When she excused herself to go to the toilet, I could see all those eyes, lit by candlelight, in that darkened restaurant following her all the way to the door. The faces of the women were the funniest. They leaked the most. They must have thought that nobody could see them. They were off guard. I could see their expressions by the light of those candles. Pure emotional leakage. Just pure envy. It felt good to be with such a desirable woman. She had a confidence in the way that she walked.

We stayed off the subject of my brother for most of the night, even though to begin with I was desperate to hear her talk about him, to get a little of him back for myself through somebody else's memories. But perhaps I was worried about what she might say. I didn't want to hear her say that he was the biggest and best lover that she had ever had. I definitely didn't want to hear any of that. I didn't want to be compared with him. I didn't want to hear how funny, or how charismatic, or how charming he was. I had heard all that so many times before from my mother and from everybody else.

So even though we both knew that we were there to talk about him, that this was the whole point of our date, we somehow avoided it. It was as if she could sense somehow that any deep sharing or any deep revelations were to be avoided. I don't know how she sensed this. Perhaps, she was very intuitive, perhaps she could read men well.

We just alluded to little things about him. We skimmed the surface using fragments of his life as stones on a deep, bottomless lake. His smile, the scar on his left knee, his laugh when he was embarrassed, and we would sit back happy and content that we had a common point of reference in our different journeys through the vagaries of life.

At times, I could see in her eyes exactly what he had meant to her. She didn't have to say it. If the truth be known, I didn't want her to say it any more explicitly. Her eyes were explicit enough.

These common points of reference, just touched upon, anchored his biography and she and I together in that quiet moonlit sea with the reflection of the candle off the glass table top. They gave us a reason to be there, and that was enough for me.

And as the night wore on, I started to feel that I didn't really want to hear him even mentioned. I was enjoying the moment too much. He was gone. It was me here now. With her.

I told her all about me, all about my life at Cambridge and at times she looked a little puzzled and confused. From time to time, I thought that she was going to say something, she would hunch up ready to talk but then relax again, as if the moment had passed. She would sit back quiet again and smile, as if I had explained something to her, something that she was now under-standing for the first time.

But then again Cambridge was an odd and disorienting expe-rience. It needs a lot of explaining.

The night passed too quickly for either of us, I thought. She kept me occupied with her tales of life in the North, and some of the characters that lived up here. And many of them sounded just like characters rather than real people. 'Ten bob millionaires', friends of the stars, hangers-on playing terrible disjointed roles to be somebody still, in a city where the mines and the steelworks were all closing down. 'To survive,' she said. 'Just to survive.'

I didn't want the evening to end and was disappointed when she asked the waiter to call a taxi, which came far too quickly.

She kissed me gently on my lips in the taxi home. 'You're nice,' she said. 'Very nice.' I remembered for some reason at that very instant my French teacher at school telling me off for translating 'jolie' as 'nice'. 'What does nice mean for God's sake?' he asked. 'It's so tepid, so bloody vague.' I had never heard him swear before. It had always stuck in my mind. But why it came back to me at that very instant I don't know.

I didn't want to be nice, tepid, and vague. I wanted to be … wanted. I wanted to be like my brother, I suppose. At that very moment, I wanted to be *him*. It was just a feeling.

Just an intense, burning sort of feeling to be the man with the thick wad of girls' telephone numbers, scribbled in thick eye liner, bulging in his inside pocket.

And that was it, as far as I was concerned. I had fallen through some trap door, and emerged falling into a world of blinding light. My brother, I think, if I had managed to think about him at all, would still have been on the surface of that older greyer world that I had now left behind. The world that I had now left behind quite suddenly and without any planning or reflection whatsoever.

# TWELVE

It was late in the afternoon, so late that all of the windows of the student tower had lit up in front of me like rows of noughts and crosses on a game show. I could see small dark figures moving against the light. Some may have been watching me. I couldn't tell. I didn't really care. I had been seeing Adele for about two months and this was a glorious time. She would ring me in the afternoons and make me laugh so loudly that people would pop their heads around my office door to check if I was okay.

Adele worked long but irregular hours. So we saw each other whenever we could. 'You should be at bloody work,' Robert my housemate would say. 'Count yourself bloody lucky to have a job.' But he was just jealous, and anyway I was getting the work done. I was working hard. I deserved some time off.

I watched a long, delicate index finger trail across my white screen. It was a metaphoric gesture that I had observed illustrating the concept of 'realizes'. The index finger was rising like a missile into the air illustrating an idea coming from nowhere. It was the concept of realization beautifully portrayed by that hand in front of me. I was writing down my description in long hand, plotting its intricate trajectory, and thinking of Adele, and the trajectory of my desire.

Suddenly the phone rang. I pressed the pause button on my video. It was Stanley the porter. There was somebody on the way up to see me. He didn't know who he was. But whoever it was wouldn't wait until I came down to fetch him, which was the rule to prevent strangers wandering around the department.

There was a loud knock on the door, and no wait for any response. The door swung open and hit the wall, some chipped plaster started its own trajectory to the floor. It was Lenny. He invited himself in.

'You didn't think that you could hide from me forever,' he said sitting on my armchair. 'I thought that I'd just pop in to see you,' he said smiling. 'I was up this way anyway. I was just passing.' And then after a pause. 'The way you do.'

He looked around the room in a slow, deliberate fashion, almost theatrically. 'Do you always sit in the bloody dark?' he asked trying to make it sound funny. He switched on the light. 'Let's throw some light on the subject. Eh?'

I hadn't said anything yet. I was very surprised to see him. I didn't think that he knew where I worked. His eyes fixated on my screen.

'So what's this all about?' he asked, pointing at the hand movement, frozen in the middle of its meaningful trajectory.

'It's my research on hand movement,' I said. 'This is what I study.'

'Oh,' he said.

'This is what I do,' I said. There was a long pause, as he continued to stare at the screen as if he had missed something.

'How's Linzi?' I asked. I thought that it was polite to ask.

'Still knocking about. Still out every night enjoying herself,' said Lenny.

'How's your new friend? A mate of mine saw the two of you out. He didn't know who she was but he said that she was a bit tasty.'

'You don't know her,' I said.

'Do you want to bet?' said Lenny. 'I know everybody.' I shrugged my shoulders as if to say 'whatever'. He went back to looking at the gesture. 'Linzi, for one, wasn't that impressed with you,' he said in an attempt to get me going.

'Oh really,' I said with just a trace of irritation in my voice.

'Yeah, she thought that you were a bit of a useless fucker,' he said. 'Not much of a sense of humour. I said that you were probably alright. Just a bit shy.'

'But she said,' he continued, 'that you didn't seem to know much for a psychologist.'

'It's not that I don't know a lot,' I said, the irritation now fragmenting the fluency of my speech. 'It's just that I don't like to blow my own … trumpet.'

'Oh,' he said, pleased with himself for managing to irritate me so easily. 'So that's why you have so little to say for yourself. You don't like to blow your own trumpet. So you're a man of action rather than a big mouth? Is that it? That's not what Linzi told me.'

'I don't mean it that way,' I said. 'I meant in terms of my work.'

'Oh,' said Lenny. 'Really?'

I got up and walked across to the shelves and picked up a copy of 'glasses with foot out front' and put it on the video. He sat in front of me and made himself comfortable. 'Do you mind if I smoke?' he asked. I said that I did, but he ignored me. He blew the smoke towards the middle of the room for good measure. Roughly in my direction.

'Why don't you watch this carefully,' I said. I played a tiny fragment of tape and then paused the tape, and asked him what he had seen. I asked him to tell me exactly what he had seen.

'Let me see,' said Lenny, scrutinizing the screen with that look of his. 'What did I see? Hmmmm. What exactly did I see?' He was imitating my accent. 'I saw a spoilt fucker, a bit on the tubby side. Is it alright to say that? Is it alright to use ordinary language here?'

I nodded. 'In your own words,' I said. 'I wouldn't want you to try to change just for me.'

'Good. Okay then.' He changed his position on the chair.

'Probably a public-school boy, like you.' He pointed at me in a sharp jabbing movement with the hand holding the cigarette, and screwed his lower jaw up.

'A bit of a swot. A bit boring looking, like a lot of university types,' he said.

'Anything else?' I enquired. 'What about the gesture?' I played the short loop of tape again.

'Yes, there's definitely a gesture there. A little bit of hand movement. Yes, I can see that. He's nervous. Is that what you're after? Yes, I can tell that. He's definitely nervous.'

Suddenly a new expression swept across his face. 'Oh, I've got it. Is he a pouf or something? A bum bandit? Is that what the gesture is meant to tell me? Is he a bit on the old limp-wristed side? That's it. He's a fucking bum boy. You've devised a new technique for spotting poufs. That would be very useful for the police or the army. You could make millions from your research.'

I rolled my eyes to the smoky ceiling of my room in an exaggerated way and said that it wasn't anything to do with his sexuality. I tried again. 'What about what the gesture is saying?' He looked again. 'Not much,' he said. 'Now listen to the speech this time.' I played the tape with the sound turned up. 'She's eating the food,' said the overweight public schoolboy with the limpish wrist in front of us. 'Now watch the tape again,' I said. 'Now what is the gesture saying?' 'Nothing,' said Lenny. 'Except that he's a nervous pouf.' 'Okay. Let me ask you a few questions about it.' 'Fire away,' said Lenny, who had obviously decided to humour me. 'He says that "she's eating the food". What is she eating?' I asked. 'Something like a sandwich?' said Lenny. 'How big is this sandwich?' I asked.
'Pretty big,' he said.

'How is she eating it?'

'The fucking normal way,' he said. 'That's a queer fucking question. Using her fucking feet, of course. Don't be so fucking daft.'

'Okay forgetting about the last one,' I said 'you see you got some information from the gesture. You knew that it was a sandwich. You knew that it was big. Just look at the original cartoon.' I dropped it onto my desk in front of him. 'Look at what she is eating,' I said. 'You got both answers right, even though the fat boy never mentioned any of this in what he was saying. Do you see the significance of this?'

'Not really,' said Lenny.

'Look,' I said. 'Speech and gesture work together to tell you about what is going on out there in the world. Speech doesn't give you the full picture. He never said in his speech - "she's eating a sandwich". His gesture told you what she was eating. Look at the cartoon from the Beano. Look at this picture. What's Ivy eating? That's right. It's a sandwich - a big sandwich.'

'Oh,' said Lenny.

'Gesture is a window on the human mind,' I said. I could feel myself getting almost emotional, the speech was cracking a little. A mistake when you are with the likes of Lenny. It gives him an advantage. 'Do you understand what I am saying here?' I asked. He sat there looking at me long and hard then his face started to light up as if he had just thought of something.

'Do you mean to say that you get paid for doing this? I'm in the wrong fucking game,' he said. 'I'm in the wrong fucking racket.'

I realized that it was impossible. I thought of that metaphoric gesture again, the one that rises from the ground into the air. The one that can signify 'realization'. I didn't make any gesture. I just sat there.

'Honestly, I'm in the wrong fucking game,' he said again.

'Okay, I'll show you something else,' I said. I led him into a less used, dustier room where there was some equipment for physiological measurement. A device for measuring galvanic skin response and a slide projector and a long mirror stretching along one wall. It was equipment for an older study, long before my time at the university.

'This is more like it,' he said. 'Is this lie detection or something like that? I can identify with that kind of work.'

I said that it was something like that.

I made him sit on a red plastic chair in the middle of the room, and I attached the electrodes to his large horny hands and explained that I was going to record his galvanic skin response to certain stimuli which would produce a variety of emotional responses in him. I activated a hidden video camera behind the one-way mirror to film his facial expression, without telling him, of course. He sat there with this smile on his face that didn't waver. 'Try to relax,' I said.

'I am fucking relaxed,' he replied. The first image burst into life front of him. It was a mother and a new-born infant, a beatific look on the mother's face.

'Aaaah,' he said. 'Am I allowed to make comments like this to show that I'm normal?'

'Not really,' I said. 'It will affect the equipment.'

'Okay then I'll say it to myself instead. Aaaah,' he said again. It wasn't any quieter the second time around.

'Look, you have to be silent for this experiment to work,' I said.

The next image appeared in front of him. It was of a landscape, a mountainous landscape. I could feel my own emotion changing in very personal ways that few psychologists, who did not know about my brother, would have understood. I recognized the landscape. It was the Alps with Mont Blanc in the background. My brother had climbed there one summer. I had kept the postcard from him safe. One of the few tangible things I had from him. I would look at the signature and imagine him signing the card in the Alpine sun and I would sometimes cry quietly to myself. It was a good device for eliciting hurt. A handy little weapon when I wanted to cut myself with an emotional scalpel.

'Oooooh, that's a nice picture,' he said. 'Very peaceful.'

'Look,' I said quietly, 'I'm not trying to see if you're normal through what you say. Just try to be silent.'

The next picture was of a naked woman.

'Nice,' he said. 'I know that I'm not allowed to comment, but I don't want you to think that I'm a queer fucker like that other cunt. That's very nice. Nice big fucking tits.'

He made wet smacking noises with his lips, like a baby sucking. 'You can tell that I'm normal,' he said.

The next image was a graphic photograph of somebody butchered in some atrocity or other in Africa. The victim was black. It was a scene of some tribal slaughter. It was an extreme image. There was a lot of blood. His head drowning in a deep pool of blood on a dusty track. It looked like a machete attack, deep slashes everywhere. I hadn't selected the photographs. I wouldn't ask strangers to watch this. They belonged to somebody else. They were designed to produce extreme emotional responses in people. I had heard about students viewing this particular picture and covering their eyes. Shielding themselves from the horrors of life.

I watched Lenny's face. He seemed to be staring more intently at this picture, taking it all in. He didn't say anything. Perhaps he had got bored with goading me. His pupils seemed to have opened up like flowers in the rain.

The images went on and on. He sat there often smirking, sometimes staring a little more intently, masking as much as he could with that great irritating smile of his because he suspected that there was something or somebody behind the mirror.

'So what did you learn about me, Mr. Psychologist?' he asked at the end of the sequence. 'Am I normal?' He looked at me. I gave a gentle cultured laugh.

'Pretty normal,' I said. 'For somebody in your profession.'

He didn't seem to like my response. 'So what did you learn through all of that bollocks?' he asked. 'That I can smile even when I see a dead body? I could have told you that if you'd asked me. It's a hard world out there, mate, I've seen more than most.'

I told him that it wasn't as simple as that. I took him into another room with equipment for playing the video tape back in slow motion. I made him sit down as I rewound the tape and found a short sequence. I played his own recording back to him. He didn't look surprised that he had been taped. He assumed that everybody deceived whenever they could. I showed him *his* face in close-up during those first few nanoseconds when the image first appeared.

I explained to him that there are tell-tale signs of emotion in the human face, but that these are usually missed by observers because of their fleeting nature. I showed him his own micro-expressions, this large fleeting image now ticking slowly across the monitor a frame at a time. His face slowed down sufficiently for us all to see.

'People never see these expressions of yours,' I said. 'But I can.' I was sounding almost as arrogant as him. I glanced up at him. He was looking interested in what I had to say. He was off guard now.

I went through his performance frame by frame right in front of him, isolating the micro-expressions of disgust and surprise and other expressions of fear and sadness before he managed to squelch them with that great smirking smile of his in place. That great mask of his, behind which he hid so often.

He was impressed by what I had managed to uncover. He was laughing at his own slightly inadequate performance. All there on the screen in front of him. His mask not quite quick enough, not quite as quick as he had always thought.

'I'm still better than the rest, eh?' he said. 'I know that.' I didn't answer. I felt that I had the knowledge now. 'I'm still good, doc?' he asked. He sounded unsure of himself for the first time ever. 'Isn't that true?'

'Sort of,' I said. I felt that I had turned the tables on him. I could be non-committal now. The one with the brief vague comments that had to be attended to.

'Well, doc,' he said. 'It just shows you. We've all got our fucking uses.'

And he left with that vague comment ringing in my ears that had me wondering for the rest of the day.

# THIRTEEN

It was six months later and I was out late. Again. It was a quarter past two in the morning and it was nearly time for the changeover. One shift off, one shift on. That's how it worked. They weren't really shifts, but that's what they called them. I suppose that they thought that they were back in the steel mills. We were the late shift.

Adele hadn't arrived yet. I was still waiting. This was *The Venue,* even more up-market than Lenny's club. More style city, that's what they said. The late shift, the men in the know, the faces with the good connections, called it *The Ven.*

A quarter past two. I knew the exact time without looking at my watch. I had developed a sort of internal clock that worked well at night, an internal clock that ticked away nicely in the dark. You can't keep looking at your watch in a place like this, a place like *The Ven.* People might think that you were bored. It was just another little trick that I had picked up along the way in waiting for Adele.

I knew the time because I sensed that the bar had been closed for about fifteen minutes. I had got a drink in just before that. You had to make this one last while the bouncers got the punters out of the club. The ordinary punters, I mean.

The flat lager sat in my glass. I looked down at it. The last bubbles swimming in the middle of the glass looked a bit like the shape of a map of Sri Lanka. I laughed quietly and sipped the flat lager. I looked back inside again. The map seemed to have changed. The remaining bubbles were breaking up. That's presumably what happens to bubbles. They don't dissolve - they break up, osmosis or something like that literally tears them apart. The island with nice neat boundaries in the middle of my glass had gone. I scanned the circumference of the glass, but there was not a single bubble left.

I was trying to fill my time, without looking around me, without making eye contact and starting up a conversation. I wanted to be on my own at the changeover. You hear about drinkers crying into their glass, but I had noticed that a lot of punters spend a good deal of their time just staring down into the bottom of it. It's a kind of civil way of not attending to all the stuff going on around you. It says to the punters out there 'look, I'm counting bubbles, fuck off.'

The drink tasted metallic in my mouth. It does when you sip it like that. That's not how lager is meant to be drunk. That's what the owner of the club liked to say to me. He'd catch me sitting with a dribble of honey-coloured liquid in my glass, more spit than lager, and make his little comment. That always made me laugh.

The two waitresses in the wine bar - Sandra and Michelle in their fishnet tights and leotards had cashed up and had just finished stacking the glasses. They looked bored. They wore tired expressions which rarely changed. Too tired to change the configuration of their faces from one moment to the next. Their interaction was all very impersonal, professional they might call it. There was no eye contact, not even with each other, as if they were focused on the job in hand. But they weren't, and you knew it.

Every punter in the wine bar that night probably had similar thoughts. You could see it in their faces. Leers creeping across from the eyes to the mouth and then out to the further edges of the face, and then just sort of hanging there. Adele liked to say that punters leaked their emotions and their desires and their feelings like rusty buckets. All men just wanted one thing. She said that she knew that through working in the beauty business. Men sometimes used her sunbeds. Vain men, like the men who used sunbeds, were the worst of all.

But that's not what I saw. It wasn't the leaking that was important, it wasn't the fact that these feelings got out in the first place. Rather it was the fact that these expressions, which told you all you needed to know about what they were thinking, stayed there on their face for far too long. That's what gave the game away. It was all to do with time. These ordinary punters wore their feelings like old tired suits. It was like having a dirty stopover, and going out without changing on a Sunday afternoon in Saturday's best clobber. Everybody would be able to read you like a book; everybody would be able to tell exactly what you'd been up to.

Old tired suits, that's all that girls like Sandra and Michelle and Adele ever saw. Leers locked into inebriated faces, with a few faltering words following these unblinking, unchanging expressions into the space between the punter and her. I was now better at disguising my thinking than most, and when I did leak the odd feeling, I would notice it quickly, and begin the process of burying it. Burying it alive.

I was learning.

Sandra wore fishnet stockings and a leotard cut very high above her fishnet tights. It was a come-on to justify the higher prices up here in the wine bar. I would pay her a compliment when she was down fetching a glass from the lower shelf and watch her look up at me, smiling. The ordinary punter never got that. It was hard to get a smile from Sandra, even when she was happy, which itself was a rarity. If you ever tried chatting to her, she would quite readily tell you all about her miserable home life, as long as you weren't leering at her. She lived with her mother, whom she didn't get on with. She had a little girl called 'Sam' or sometimes 'Sami', with an 'i', depending on her mood, who her mother looked after when she was out working. She would be home just after three in the morning to see Sami lying there, her sheets kicked all over the place, having fled from the monsters in her dreams. Sunbeam her *My Little Pony* with sharp dark teeth chasing her through bright green meadows, green like the backs of plastic chairs melted and shiny. Sami's hair stuck to her fore-head, pyjamas wrinkled and wet. All those wicked dreams in Sandra's absence, all that kicking and running whilst Sandra served cocktails with names that might sound funny on holiday, but just sounded ridiculous now on a cold night in the centre of Sheffield in the middle of a recession.

'Sex on the beach', it said on the black board beside the bar. But it didn't sound quite right here when you had to say it out loud. The punters just pointed up at the blackboard on the wall. 'Two of those,' they'd say. They called the club 'Style City', some-times. 'Two of those big yellow drinks with the straws sticking out of them, luv,' they'd say. 'Real Style City.'

The cashing up usually took about half an hour. There were one or two stragglers left in the wine bar, one was talking to Fat Eddie, hoping that somehow he'd be mistaken for a VIP and asked to stay behind with the select few. But Pat never made that kind of mistake. He and Becksy were working the wine bar. The final sweep, they called it. They were professionals. 'Wine bar clear,' they would shout half jokingly when they had finished. Becksy had been in the army once. He said the lingo sticks with you forever. The bomb squad, the S.A.S., the Marines, they all had their specialized vocabularies. Becksy liked borrowing words from wherever he could. He was always trying to get me to teach him some psychological words, so that he could throw those around as well. But I didn't want to hear my words used like that.

Pat waited patiently whilst Eddie and his new friend finished talking. Eddie kept looking Pat's way, as if to say 'I'm just being polite here. Chuck him out if you like. He means nothing to me.'

But Pat was politer than that, he waited for a suitable juncture, and then in measured tones asked him to leave.

It was only the most select of the VIP's who could stay behind. The Gold Card holders.

Everybody knew who we were. The Gold Card didn't actually exist, or if it did, I'd never actually seen one. Perhaps, Adele had one secretly stashed away in her handbag. I don't know. I never knew why she was a VIP. Connections, I suppose. It wasn't what you knew around here. That's what they said.

They called us the queue jumpers behind our backs, and worse, much worse. Flash bastards, poseurs, ten bob millionaires, but they missed the point. We didn't pretend to be millionaires, just men in the know. I was waiting for Adele. It was as simple as that. I was a man in the know.

We were queue jumpers though. You see that the first thing that you came across when you were looking for this particular night-club was the queue. This place was almost defined by its queue. 'Oh, that's the club where you have to queue to get in,' they'd say. 'The club with the strict door policy. The club where you have to queue all night.'

The queue usually stretched out from the door down towards the steps below, and right along the glass office block. A long, entropic line, oozing anticipation and quite often desperation. The bouncers could seem quite whimsical some nights, but they weren't whimsical, just thorough. It was enough just to get into the place. Some nights you could queue for an hour or more. A significant part of the night was spent out there in the dark hoping that you looked the part sufficiently to get the nod from the bouncers to get into the club. It was hard for ordinary punters to know how to dress because a significant part of the evening was to be spent in the wind and the rain, and yet a coat necessitated queuing at the end of the night, and if you've pulled the last thing you want to do is more queuing. So most punters arrived without coats and stood in flimsy dresses or shirts even in the cruelest of months.

The queue always started early. It had been long that particular night. Just the way that we VIP's, with our gold cards, are supposed to like it. They say that it feels marvelous to walk right up past them - the respectable citizens of this fine old town, all queuing in the frigging rain. Soaked to the bloody skin. I still found it very embarrassing trying to jump the queue. You can feel all these eyes in your back, like daggers where somebody is twisting and turning the blade in between your shoulder blades.

That night though the door staff had got everything in hand. They had managed to get the ordinary punter right up against the wall of the building, leaving this little space to the right. This space is important. It gives the doormen a chance to see past the ordinary punter. They can then watch you as you arrive, and nudge the ordinary punters even closer to the wall. Just enough room to squeeze in, in front of the paying customer. The mugs, Adele called them, standing freezing in the rain.

On a good night, or a bad night depending upon how you looked at these things, you would know everyone in the club. Tonight, Fat Eddie was in his favourite spot, just to the right of the edge of the top bar. I got my Rolex watch off him. Nineteen quid it cost. Of course, it wasn't real. But it looked the part, in here, in this dim light You could only tell that it was snide when you took it off. If you took it off, that is. It was as light as a feather. But you never take it off, except in bed.

'Then it's too late.' That's what Fat Eddie always said. 'Far too late. You're already in there.' I hated the way that he talked to Adele, he was always leering at her. He was always making her laugh. 'If you make a bird laugh,' he would say to me some nights when I was waiting for her, 'You're halfway in there.'

Adele said that he was okay. 'He's harmless, really. Quite funny as well. He makes me laugh.'

I always hated her saying that, as if she was confessing something to me. Fat Eddie was always angling for this or that. Some fishy deal or other. Or he was trying to land some gentle, wide-eyed, creature, who would be flapping helplessly in mid-air in front of him. 'I've got another one on tonight,' he would say. 'Get the landing net ready.' And he would make a little reeling gesture, or sometimes his right hand would hold the net out. It always got a laugh from the men in the know. Sometimes he would make a gesture showing the landed fish being cracked against the back of his boot. You could almost hear the thud; the gesture was that clear. The noise of the death. The fish well and truly fucked, as Eddie liked to say. Then you knew what that wide-eyed thing was in for. He had got her.

Sometimes I would go to Lenny's club instead for a break from Fat Eddie and his jokes and his barbed humour. I had got to know Lenny better over the months. I was starting to learn how to handle him. To survive in his presence. I knew what to talk about to keep him from having a go at me. Most of the time. Lenny, I had decided, wasn't so bad deep down inside. But Adele didn't like it there. That's what she said. Too common for her.

Some nights Fat Eddie would have five or six snide watches on one arm. You could see the bulge in his shirt. He liked to keep them covered. He didn't need to sell them. He just did it for pin money. Beer money. I had heard that he was into passing off counterfeit notes at the moment, but that was just a rumour. But a reliable one.

You didn't need to have money to have style. That was what they would say in the club. It was just as well. Many of them had nothing. Just a gold pass.

You got to know all the other VIP's - the big hitters, and the rest. Richard was by the pillar; he was big in fire insulation for factories. He was talking to Brian. Brian owned his own hairdresser's, or he did once. I had heard that he was currently unemployed. But he could get in here for nothing, and he could make a half a lager last a very long time indeed. Some other VIP would always buy him a drink. Perhaps things were a little vague around here sometimes. But they were all superstars. For a while. Or the boyfriend of a superstar. In my case.

I was standing there, waiting patiently. The last of the ordinary punters were running around desperate for their three hours away from the wife or the husband. Their three hours of freedom. Pretending to be somebody that they were not, computer sales-man, air hostess, doctor, footballer, model, graphic designer, architect, aroma therapist, manageress at Marks and Spencer's, anything that sounds fancy and grand. But miner, steelworker, canteen girl or worse ex-miner, ex-steelworker or ex-canteen girl didn't sound quite right in Style City. These ordinary punters were into deceptions that might last the whole night. Some of the VIP's had deceptions that lasted a good deal longer.

There was Frank with his Rolls Royce parked underneath the club, with just a gallon or so of petrol in the tank. If he pulled, he had to work out exactly how many miles away she lived, to see if he could get there and back without running out of gas. That was his word. Gas. He said that it sounded more American, more glamorous. He knew all the districts in Sheffield and whether he could make it there or not on the couple of gallons of gas he had in the tank. Some nights you would see him in the car park under-neath the club siphoning a few gallons from a Ford or a Vauxhall into his tank, to give himself a bit of an edge. He told any attrac-tive girl that he met that he was looking for an au pair for his chil-dren. The fact that his children were both adults and never spoke to him was never mentioned. But Frank looked the part.

'The man with the five octane smile,' is how he described himself. White flashing teeth that he liked to expose. He would bring a little phial of water with him and brush his teeth in the underground car park just before entering the night-club. Great slabs of newly-polished ivory glinting in the dark of the club. VIP's who knew him called him 'the man with the five octane breath'. He told us all that he was an entrepreneur. He had started trading cars from home - Vauxhall to Ford back to Vauxhall to

Nissan to old BMW to old Merc to old Roller. He wasn't making any money, but he was getting some cheap thrills through his business dealings. He was addicted to business. That's how he described it.

Sometimes Frank lost money. He took his family on holiday to Skegness and came back in a hearse. He traded his Vauxhall Carlton for the hearse. 'The art of the deal,' he called it. He tried to sell the hearse to a sandwich shop outside Barnsley. He suggested the advertising slogan - 'People are dying for our beef sandwiches.' They didn't go for it. So he tried a local butcher's instead, and a new slogan. 'People are dying for our Barnsley chop.' They bought the idea and the hearse and his career was launched. He was an entrepreneur now.

He kept the Roller to give him an edge in business. 'I want people to know who they are dealing with,' he said. 'It doesn't matter who you are, you know, or where you come from. That's what Mrs. Thatcher says. There's no law against us Northerners doing well.' He had just spent the last four months collecting pig meal bags for profit. His brother who kept pigs had suggested this to him. 'Some of the best entrepreneurial ideas come second-hand,' he had told me. 'It doesn't matter where you get the idea from, as long as it's a little gem, a little corker.'

He used the same language to describe women. Little gem, little corker, and at the end of the evening he would be out there looking for any wee bargains left. Wee bargains or cheap goods. Anything when he was desperate. No matter how damaged or soiled.

In the four months since he became the self-declared pig bag king of South Yorkshire he had collected two thousand pig meal bags. 'Half a ton - a mountain of bags in a field at the bottom of my garden,' he said. 'I used to sit in my kitchen and look at all that money I was accumulating. The neighbours were all ringing the council to complain, but I think that they were just jealous of my success. I was thinking about what I was going to spend all my money on.' A mountain of pig meal bags was growing; he would watch this organic process from his kitchen. 'It was almost too easy,' he had said. 'Capitalism is as natural as farming,' he would say. That day he had sold the pig meal bags. He got sixty quid for the lot. 'Less than four pounds a week for all of my effort.' He was drinking tonic water in the club that night. He said that he had a queasy tummy.

But Frank was still a millionaire in here, in the club with little lights on the carpet like those on an aircraft floor to guide you to safety in the event of an emergency. Lights to follow when the power goes, lights to follow in the dark. The Roller was underneath the club. Frank lied for years. He was still a budding, thrusting entrepreneur. In here, at least.

'Mrs. Thatcher knows that it's all to do with luck,' he would say. 'You don't necessarily need brains. I know lots of millionaires and none of them are brain surgeons.' He used the word 'brains' a lot. 'You've got brains,' he said, 'your bird's got brains. I've got a little savvy.' He always wanted me to say that he had got brains as well, but I never did. I tried to be honest even here.

I was taking it nice and steady that night watching the few remaining ordinary punters make their moves and the professionals out having to deal with them. I was watching Dave, a deaf bouncer, in action down on the main floor. He had a large mop of curly blond hair on a big open face, and a dinner jacket that was too tight. It was buttoned up, and stretched across his ample torso. You could see that he was angry even in the neon glow of the night-club. The flushing of his face might not have been visible, but the facial musculature was stretched as tight as his jacket. He was standing in between two punters who had been having a slanging match. The punters had both stood their ground, moving neither this way nor that, but their heads had started to tilt slowly towards each other, until now only inches separated them. Dave had to move into that gap. In the seconds that it had taken him to get there, he had to make a snap decision.

THE BODY'S LITTLE SECRETS

One had to be his focus. Not the bigger of the two, but the little one, the mouthy one. The little one whose face was twisting and contorting.

'Read my lips,' Dave's mouth pouted and protruded in accentuated fashion. No sound came. The little guy with the cream shirt and black waistcoat and the big mouth looked quizzical. It was as if the bouncer in the tight jacket was echoing his own exaggerated social performance.

'What?' he said. Dave went through the motions more slowly this time. 'Read my lips.' The man in the cream shirt thought that the bouncer was winding him up. 'Do - you - want - to - leave?' said Dave. Each word came out with a large gap in between, so that there was no overall rhythm in even the facial action of the delivery. Dave pointed towards the door to bring the point home. Well not so much towards the door as at the ladies' toilet, but down past the ladies' toilet, there was undoubtedly an exit. Dave watched for small subtle cues of understanding in the face of this small mouthy man, but saw none. He repeated the gesture, this time making a low guttural sound from deep within. 'You,' he said. This time he used his index finger to take the man in the cream shirt on a more detailed journey down past the side entrance of the bar where some VIP's clustered, down past the queue to the ladies' toilet, out past the cloakroom attendant, and right into the cold misty air outside. His index finger made a short sharp stabbing movement at the end, a stab into the smoky air of the club. This was to represent the expulsion into the cold sharp air. The coming to one's senses.

Comprehension crept slowly and deliberately across his face. Starting in the eyes, down across his jaw and mouth and back up to the top of his head. He nodded slowly. 'I'm sorry. I didn't realize that you couldn't talk. Here let me shake your hand. I was just having a few words that's all. Hey, let me shake his hand as well. No problems. Sorry about that. Let me buy you a drink. Oh sorry, it's a pity that you can't drink when you're working.'

So many words filled the warm balmy air of smoke and perfume, words about desire and social status, words to persuade and cajole, words that lied and fabricated, and Dave could hear none of them. I was sure that sometimes he was glad. He didn't have to listen to all of this.

I pushed my way past a few VIP's, now swaying gently in their alcohol induced haze, and headed towards the toilet. The toilet attendant was looking harassed, as the ordinary punters about to leave tried to spray themselves with the aftershave sitting out for them, without paying the customary twenty pence. The aftershave was twice as dear here as at Lenny's club.

'Come on lads, it's twenty pence a shot. I've got plenty of change. Only the best gear here. Real fanny magnet stuff,' said Tom, as after shave dispensers fired off indiscriminately into the surrounding ether. 'One spray per payment, please,' shouted Tom. 'One shot each. I'm counting. Hey, sonny, you've had five squirts of Paco Rabanne. That's a quid so far. I hope you can afford that.'

He winked at me as I went into the toilet. 'You can have three squirts of whatever you like free of charge.' He pushed some Kouros my way. I didn't like the smell of this after shave, it was too sweet and sickly for me, but I was too polite to refuse it. I squeezed the nozzle three times as directed. 'Three's plenty,' said Tom. 'You don't want to overpower that bird of yours with your smell, when she gets here. Do you?'

I went back to the wine bar and I drained the last drop of my flat lager from my glass. Fat Eddie was still talking away to his new friend.

'Oh, are you coming as well?' the anonymous punter asked Eddie. He was trying to sound sincere. But this punter knew what went on alright. He knew the club wasn't really closing. Who really goes home at half past two in the morning? 'No, I'll be out in a minute,' said Eddie. 'In a minute.'

Then I saw him look towards the entrance. Something had caught his eye. 'Here she comes,' he said. 'The most beautiful girl in Sheffield. Miss Yorkshire TV.' She walked in, up the steps and kissed me on the lips with a loud 'mmmmhmmmmpph' noise. The smell of her perfume was overpowering. She was wearing a tight black dress. It was very short. 'I need a drink,' she said. I could smell a hint of gin on her breath. She had brushed her teeth. I sometimes wondered what kind of club it was that allowed the receptionists to have a drink like that, and then brush their teeth on the premises before they left.

'Aren't there any gentlemen, here?' she asked. She tried to sound like Marilyn Monroe. She emitted a high-pitched squeal. It sounded like a pig being stuck. I never liked that noise she made. It was one of the few things that I didn't like about her.

'I'm a right good actress,' she always said. 'I have to be. I can do Marilyn Monroe and Ava Gardner.'

'Aren't there any gentlemen here?' she repeated, she tried it in a deeper voice this time.

'At this time of night,' said Fat Eddie, leaning forward on his stool to look down her top. 'You must be kidding.'

And the late shift all burst out laughing. And so did I. Eventually.

# FOURTEEN

It was the next night in a wine bar that I contacted Lenny to enlist his help in the analysis of the video-recording of the killing in the drinking club. My professor had given me the tape to analyze. He had been spreading the word about the forensic possibilities of our exciting new research on human body language. A defense solicitor, a friend of a friend in his extensive west-side of Sheffield network full of dinner parties and burgundy, had contacted him and enquired if a psychological analysis of the tape could potentially reveal whether the murder *victim* was behaving aggressively in any way. Could the defendant have felt intimidated or frightened by the victim's behaviour in the moments leading up to the critical event? Could the defendant have been feeling under threat? In other words, could the victim, in any way, have contributed to this tragic event and his own demise? My professor slowly explained to me how important it was to conduct a thorough and compelling analysis. He left me in no doubt about the importance of getting it right. 'I told him that my young assistant studied at Cambridge,' he said. 'That did the trick.'

That was why I had been given the tape. I only managed to get Lenny to come by telling him what was on the tape, but I got him to swear that he wouldn't mention it to anybody. I thought that he might be able to provide some valuable assistance. After all, he was used to studying encounters in the various clubs where he worked; he was used to analyzing and interpreting the behaviours of drunk, violent ... common punters. I'd never studied body language beyond the laboratory, and to be honest I'd never even studied the common man. And, if the truth be told, I didn't want to watch a murder on my own, despite all of the warnings on the legal paperwork about confidentiality, and its repeated emphasis that this video-recording was 'for my eyes only'. I wouldn't have been able to sit through a tape knowing that this person - this ordinary, everyday bloke, perhaps a bit tipsy, in great vivid, close-up detail on the screen in front of me, was going to lose their life by the end of the tape. Lenny, however, had no such qualms and was clearly excited at the propect; he agreed to come that very night. Adele was working again.

The video-recoding left me feeling queasy, and with a sort of immutable generalized anxiety that was hard to pinpoint and impossible to shift.

The following night, I arranged to meet Adele in the club late after she had finished work. I don't know what *really* caused the argument. Perhaps I was tired, perhaps she was. But I know what sparked it off. She told me on the way home in the taxi that she had to work *again* the following night. It was the third night in a row. Her job at the nightclub in Chesterfield was just meant to be part-time. I told her that she didn't make enough time for me. She asked me if I wanted her to be like the rest of them - ten bob millionaires, skint, acting big.

'I'm a grafter,' she said. 'I always have been.'

'Why can't I pop in to your club to see you?' I asked.

'It's too far away just to pop in, but I'll take you one day,' she said. 'And anyway, the boss doesn't like friends popping in to see his staff, especially not boyfriends - they're not good for business.'

I said that this wasn't good enough, and I asked the taxi to stop and I walked back to my bedsit on my own in a huff. I broke an aerial off a car on the way and tapped it on pock marked walls all the way back. I was feeling angry. She didn't ring me the next day at work, so that night I got a taxi to Chesterfield to surprise her at the club where she worked. She wasn't there, and they said that they'd never heard of her. They asked me if I was sure that I had got her name right, as if she was some casual pick-up. They didn't seem to realize that we had been going out for months now, bloody months.

I went out alone to *The Ven* and stood in the darkness with the late shift. The men with nowhere to go.

I knew in my heart that they all knew more about her than me. I wanted to ask them, but I didn't dare. I didn't talk much that night to anybody. I just stood in silence, sipping the flat lager in my glass, until my whole mouth tasted metallic and dead. They sensed that Adele and I had had an argument. They left me alone.

They were all very good at keeping secrets. Sometimes I think that it was the secrets that kept them together. Standing there a few steps above the ordinary punter with Pat or Becksy guarding their positions for them. Their positions in the club that is. They were somebody because that was where they could stand, because of who they knew and what little secrets they knew. There was no substance behind any of it. No ideology, no commitment. Just users talking their way into things. Being somebody on the basis of a few nods and winks from other Gold card holders who boasted about having numbers like 001 and 007 on their cards. The cards that nobody ever saw anyway.

So this was what has happened to the North, I thought. The substance had been removed and replaced with this. My brother had never warned me about any of it, because presumably in the mining villages and in the front line against the mounted police, he had been involved in something quite different. Or it had changed since then, after Thatcher's great victory. These were the vanquished.

It was now very late. I saw the manager with a video-tape under his arm, and I knew what they were up to. They were going to watch an edited video-tape from the security cameras. I had watched them do this before. Adele called them 'peeping Toms'.

The story was starting just above my head. I could see the bright white light, and hear Fat Eddie moving his chair to get it into a better position. There was no sound on the video. Pete, the owner, would almost certainly come a little later and do the voice over. He claimed to know the words that were actually spoken on the night of the actual encounter in a dozen or more silent films, even though he was not physically present at the scene in any of them. He had told me that he would talk to his staff afterwards whilst it was all fresh in their minds and remember the words verbatim. The bouncers all said that it was worse than being interviewed by the police.

Pete wanted the exact words spoken before, during and after any confrontation or fight. Not just the gist, he wanted the exact words plus any um's or ah's. 'If you don't get the um's and ah's it puts you right out in your timing,' he always said. If he didn't get an absolutely accurate verbatim report, then the words didn't fit, and he would get very cross. 'I'd end up looking a right cunt,' he would say.

He had a script for each film which mapped, more or less, onto what was being said, given the odd millisecond or two. Nobody in the club ever disputed these words, even the bouncers who had actually used them in the first place. We were all there after hours as his guests or his employees. It would have been impolite to say the least not to take his word for it. Perhaps even a little dangerous.

The bouncers had worked out that it was more important to provide dialogue of approximately the right duration as the original, if they couldn't remember the words actually used, so that when Pete was doing his voice-over, there would be no awkward silences where Pete had come to the end of his line but the protagonists in the original film had still something to say.

Pat had confessed to me that whenever he was interviewed by the police about any incident in the club, he had started unconsciously doing something quite similar. He was making up whole stories, imagining conversations, constructing violent threats in his head, all of which had the exact temporal properties as the original and shared almost none of the actual meanings. The official police statistics for violent crime in the area were being badly affected by this practice.

I looked up at the video-screen. A man with long permed hair was standing just outside the club. He was obviously barred. Why else would someone be standing there at that time of the night? The time and date was on the bottom left hand corner of the screen. It was eight minutes to two. Eight minutes to get back into the club and hopefully score. Just time for the smoochies, the erection section, the DJ liked to say. The man with the perm kept putting his head around the door to talk to Dave, the deaf bouncer.

'Look at that fucking loser there,' said Fat Eddie, pointing up at the screen.

I was starting to hate Fat Eddie. Sometimes, I thought that it might have been something to do with Adele. But I hoped that I disliked him because of something more important.

What was it that J.B. Priestley had once written? 'First you take their faces from 'em by calling 'em the masses and then you accuse 'em of not having any faces.' Fat Eddie just saw losers out there on the street and in the club, even when they were magnified on the video in front of him. Losers with no faces and no emotion, and no individuality and no biography. Losers who would all have loved to get where he was. In the middle of all this. In the know.

'Do you know him, Cliff?' he asked of this police inspector in the corner. 'He looks like the sort of guy who would keep your lot pretty busy. A real no-hoper. Where's Pete? I wouldn't mind hearing this one.' But Pete was busy at the far end of the club, so this slice of violent life was to be viewed in silence.

There was a light on at the top right hand corner of the foyer of the club which bathed the right hand side of the picture in bright white light. It made Dave with his fair hair look quite serene but quite ghostly. Everything in the club was bright and light, everything outside was in the dark. This punter wanted to go from the dark to the light. Why he was being prevented was not clear. He was just barred for some minor or perhaps major misdemeanour. Nobody seemed to know who he was. He would have to be a nobody to be barred. That was the logic.

The punter kept putting his head round the door, and getting a knock-back. That's what they called it a 'knock-back'. It was a nice vague term, it wasn't like being barred, it had no temporal dimension written into it. If you were barred, you would be barred for a set period of time. If punters got barred, they would want to know how long they were barred for. If you got a knock-back, you couldn't legitimately enquire about the duration.

Plus, it had no motive as part of its sense. You could have a knock-back on a whim or something vaguely remembered by the door personnel. You didn't have to really justify a knock-back if you were a bouncer. You just had to be resolute for the duration of one evening. Just one evening. 'Come back tomorrow,' the bouncer would say, 'and we'll see.'

The incident on the video was just a knock-back, but it was being contested. The punter wasn't going anywhere. He was digging his heels in, metaphorically speaking, he was quite literally being a bloody nuisance. He was standing there, protesting. Breaking every rule about authority and order and who has the final say. This was worse than being a Muppet in Fat Eddie's eyes.

We all sat there watching the man with the perm. Pete had now joined us.

'Fucking asshole,' said Fat Eddie. 'If I had a knock-back I would just fuck off home. Or to another club. No offence, lads. Has that cunt got no pride?'

The man with the perm stood there outside the club, arguing away, then he flicked his cigarette into the night. It looked like a tracer going through the black night air. Some girl came out and whispered in the ear of the deaf bouncer. She kissed him on the cheek. The bouncer mouthed something after her, but because there was no sound on the video, it was hard to tell what this might be. The punter with the perm looked down the steps after the girl. He got more agitated now. He was remonstrating with the bouncer. You could see these sharp, stabbing batonic gestures emanating from him.

'He's fucking asking for it,' said Fat Eddie. 'What would you do to him, Cliff, if he was in police custody and he started pointing his finger at you like that? I bet that you would knock his lights out?' I noticed that Fat Eddie was sweating. He had also gone noticeably paler. Fat Eddie took drugs, everybody knew that. They made him sweat.

'Look that's better,' said Fat Eddie, pointing at the screen. 'He's put his hands in his pockets now. Come on Mr. Psychologist, what does that mean?'

That pale drawn face with the dark circles for eyes turned my way. The police inspector looked up from his pint of lager expectantly.

'It's hard to say,' I said. I gave a little shrug to indicate my nonchalance. It was the first time I had talked all that night.

'Hard to fucking say?' said Fat Eddie. 'Hard to fucking say?' He had pinched the muscles around his eyes to make a squinting sort of face. He rotated his head to fix eye contact with each member of the group in turn sitting in a loose sort of circle.

'Hard to fucking say?' He tried to coax a little smile from each person in turn, a smile or a laugh, like a beggar with a cap working a theatre audience. He wasn't disappointed.

'Do they pay you for these opinions up at the university?' he said. 'Hard to fucking say? Is that what you come up with when they bring some fucking nutter in to see you? "It's hard to say." And you're meant to be the expert on this. Come on Cliff, give us a professional opinion.'

He stressed the word 'professional'. 'What does the hands in the pockets mean from a professional point of view?'

Cliff set his pint of lager down slowly on the black metallic table. It made a solid clanking sound. He cleared his throat. It made him sound serious, as if the opinion he was about to express was the end-product of a great deal of deliberation. I could imagine him going through the same routine in court.

'I would say,' he began. 'I would say,' he started again in a little rhetorical flourish, 'that it means that he, the man in question, the suspect, the punter as we say around here, recognizes the seriousness of what he's got himself involved in, and that at this point in the proceedings, he's having second thoughts, serious second thoughts about continuing with his course of action.' He gave a cough to mark the end point of his testimony.

'Excellent,' said Fat Eddie. 'Fucking tremendous. You see, Mr. Psychologist, some professionals can read people like books. That was tremendous, Cliff. How did you know all that from just that one simple act?'

'Years of honest, decent police training,' said Cliff picking up his full pint mug, his pint mug that was being used against all the rules up there in the wine bar. He looked very self-satisfied with his own performance.

'Years of watching the evil bastards make their moves,' he said, 'and getting in there first before they've even made up their own minds about what nasty things to do. It gives you quite an edge on them. I can tell you that for nothing.'

'But what you've just said is not very scientific,' I said quickly and quite quietly, and I must confess without much reflection on my part.

'Not very what?' said Fat Eddie, with that squinting face of his again.

'It's not very scientific,' I said more slowly and more deliberately.

'Listen,' said Cliff, setting down his lager more forcefully this time so that a large wave of lager tipped out of the side of the glass all over the table. 'I didn't say it was scientific. I just said that it was based on years of experience. That's not the same thing.'

'What do you mean, not scientific?' asked Fat Eddie. 'It's tried and tested. That's good enough for me.

'Well, Cliff could say what he likes,' I said. 'He hasn't got a theory of what's going on here.'

'Oh I have a theory alright,' said Cliff. 'My theory is that assholes like that guy there have no bottle when it comes down to it. The drink makes them brave, but there's this little voice at the back of their mind saying "Don't fucking push it or this big bouncer here will knock your fucking lights out. Don't push your fucking luck".'

'Excellent,' said Fat Eddie. 'That's some fucking theory, that is. Does it have a name that theory of yours?'

'No,' said Cliff. 'It doesn't have any fancy psychological bollocks name. It's just a common-sense theory based on years of experience.'

'I wouldn't fancy being lifted by you, Cliff,' said Fat Eddie. 'You're too fucking clever. A man would have no chance against you.' Fat Eddie and Cliff went back to their drinking, in perfect synchrony with each other. The glasses were lifted from the table at exactly the same moment, they gulped within the same brief interval, and the glasses were put down again, all with perfect timing.

'But you can't predict anything with your theory, Cliff,' I said into the silence, breaking myself away from my observations. 'You're just offering an opinion, okay based on your experiences. But that's all it is. An opinion.'

'What?' said Fat Eddie. 'Are you saying that Cliff's theory based on his whole life's work is a load of bollocks? Is that what you are saying to his face?'

Cliff got up abruptly. He kicked the nearest stool to him away. It landed on its side, on the metallic bit of the wine bar with a clatter that rang on and on like a tinny-sounding alarm.

'What are you fucking saying?' he said. He moved across to me until he was standing just in front of me. I stayed seated.

'It's not fucking bollocks and I'll tell you why,' he said. 'The cunt with the perm is going to needle a bit more and a bit more and then he's going to get fucking decked. That's my prediction. Any cunt who needles that much deserves it. Do you understand me? Do you still think that I can't predict the future with my fucking theory?'

I nodded and tried to say that I didn't think that he could predict anything with such a theory, but the words didn't come out that easily. Fat Eddie had turned his face away from me. I was sure that he was laughing.

'Cheeky young fucker,' said Fat Eddie, when he had managed to control himself again. 'Give him a slap, Cliff.'

'Twat,' said Cliff, as he went back to pick up the stool that had fallen over.

The punter was still talking away on the video; the deaf bouncer had turned his head away. I went back to watching it. I felt my cheeks burning red. A woman in a smart suit leaving the club said something to the punter, who was still trying to talk his way in. He looked after her longingly. I found myself quite unconsciously timing this look. It was my years of training, I suppose. It was twenty-nine seconds. Nearly half a minute. That's a long time for a look of this kind. I nearly wanted to point this out to Cliff and Fat Eddie. I wanted to display to them my precision in measurement, but I looked at their faces and I guessed that they wouldn't be that interested.

On the video, you could see Pat coming up to the foyer just to check what was going on. He didn't stay long. Then Becksy came out. He had obviously been asked to have a word with the punter with the perm. You could see Pat's upturned hand gesture in the space between him and the punter, an upturned fist, open, helpless, imploring. Even this more primitive form of communication wasn't working.

If the punter had been an ape or a child he might have got the message, but he wasn't. He was a Muppet and he understood nothing. He didn't know the regulations of the club or the rules for surviving out there after dark. He didn't understand power and authority in this land of the vanquished. He didn't understand how these guys worked.

He didn't listen or attend. He was worse than ignorant. He was wilfully not attending. I wanted to make some of these observations aloud to get back in with the rest of them, all sitting there, all making comments about the action on the screen, as if they understood people. Smug, complacent bastards the lot of them.

It was now after two o'clock on the film. The club was officially closing. There was a stream of people leaving now, groups of men and gaggles of women going their separate ways. A small group of women were hanging about outside. One or two of them were smoking. You could see the bright glow from their cigarettes, the cigarettes almost alive in the dark, pulsating with the breathing in and the breathing out, with the rise and fall of the lungs. Then Big Jack arrived.

It was hard to get a sense of perspective in this shot of dark and light, but you could see that Big Jack was huge. A huge dark ominous slab in the corner of the light, behind the glass door at a slight angle. There was little expression in his face, his face was something more primitive altogether. No basic emotions ever seem to register there. Certainly no fear, but no surprise, no happiness, no anger, no disgust. Nothing of any real consequence, just a little boredom perhaps.

'This is where the film gets interesting,' said Fat Eddie, 'There's Big Jack. He's the man. He's the main man. Look at the size of that big fucker. Have you really never seen this film before, Cliff? Your prediction is awfully accurate if you haven't seen it. It is spot on actually.'

Cliff shook his head. 'No, I've never seen it.'

'But you've seen ones like it,' I said, before I could stop myself. 'You know roughly what's going to be on it. You know that the guy with the perm and the bouncer aren't going to go off hand in hand.' Cliff looked at me menacingly. He had hard narrow eyes now. Mean eyes. Colourless eyes.

Tony, one of the new glass collectors, came up to the wine bar carrying a huge number of glasses, slotted into each other. It looked like a fragile glass sculpture. He paused in front of the screen. The sculpture shook slightly. 'Fucking hell,' said Tony, unaware of our secondary conversation which had a temporary lull, as I tried to come up with an insult that wouldn't cause real offence.

'He's a giant,' said Tony. 'Is it true that he used to be a professional wrestler? Big Jack was a bit before my time. What was his wrestling name - Giant Haystacks? Godzilla? The Incredible Hulk?'

'No I think it was the Gentle Giant,' said Fat Eddie. 'I think that's what they used to call him. Six foot ten inches of pure unadulterated beef. But gentle.'

The punter stood there on the screen in front of us, trying to talk to the Gentle Giant. He held up an empty cigarette box. You could guess what he was saying. He just wanted to go in to get some cigarettes. He would only be a minute. Jack shook his large ponderous head, and looked down at his own feet, ignoring him. The punter flicked the packet at the door. The motion caught Jack's eye. You could see the eye opening wider. It was almost reptilian.

'That's done it,' said Fat Eddie. 'That's him well and truly fucked.'

'Provocative,' said Cliff. 'In the police we would describe that as very provocative.' Here we were watching all this human behaviour without the benefit of sound, and coming to all sorts of conclusions about the justifications for the violence to come, because we all knew what conclusion we were working towards. Or rather they were.

On the video, more girls came out in light summer dresses with bare legs. The punter got more agitated again. You could sense the excitement rising in our social group. We were all there now. Pete, Pat, Becksy, Fat Eddie, Cliff, Tony, Andy, and me stuck in the middle.

I had come here for answers to put me out of my misery, and here I was, watching the spectacle in front of me. Other people's misery.

There were no women left that night. Sandra and Michelle had cashed up and gone off for their taxis. They had avoided Fat Eddie. There were more words on the screen, but of course they just came across as more silent mouthing with the body activated into gesture. Some guy left carrying his coat. Then there was a pause. This was the climax of the film. I could see it in Fat Eddie's face. The smile starting. He had seen the film many times.

Suddenly from nowhere in terms of the action on the screen, this left hook erupted around the door. The punter who had had the knock-back couldn't have seen it coming. I couldn't see it coming and I had studied the whole episode up to that point in great detail. It was not in any way connected to the flow of the interaction. Some violence isn't.

I saw nothing in the video in front of me to allow me to predict Big Jack's response. Nothing. There was no sound from the screen but you could hear that punch landing. I had never heard a more solid punch. Boom. The punter went down, dead to the world. The deaf bouncer, Dave, stepped back slightly. Jack had trouble getting through the door because of his size. He had to go through sideways. The punter was off camera but you could see Jack bending over where his prostrate body must have been, waving his fist. He lifted the punter up by the shirt and punched him again. His head cracked on the paving stones.

It must have sounded like a coconut thrown onto concrete. You could almost hear the head opening up and the blood seeping out in thick gurgles.

There were two girls caught on the camera, still in the club looking out. You could see their faces. Their expressions were in marked contrast to everything else on the film. Emotion was written all over them. They were covering their faces with their hands in an attempt to hide just some of the emotional messages leaking from them. To mask just some of it.

The man who had left carrying his coat came back and said something to Big Jack. Jack gave a dismissive wave and turned away. This was perhaps the real climax to the film. This stranger dragging the punter away, dragging him backwards off-screen. The punter was out cold. He was dragging the lifeless body the way that you might drag a bag of cement. It took the same effort. The shoes of the punter with the perm scraped along the pavement. One of his shoes came off and lay in the middle of the camera shot.

I watched them all there in the club, sitting there hooting with laughter. I felt a slight disgust, but I hoped that I was managing to conceal it.

The word went down to the DJ to play the tape from the cigarette box flick again. They were commenting on that punch. It was a monster hook, a big dig, the big D, a bone cruncher, a knuckle sandwich of the highest order, a goodnight kiss from the Gentle Giant. The punch knocked the punter out. It rocked the punter, it floored the man with the glass chin, the punch travelled through the man to his boots and back.

'I felt that punch,' said Fat Eddie. 'So did I,' said Cliff.

The DJ loaded a second film into the video recorder. An Asian guy was having an argument with his wife in the doorway of the club. She was screaming in his face, but there was no sound. The camera captured it all. Fat Eddie offered to do the voice over for this one. 'You kicked my sister in the fucking fanny, you son of a bitch. Look at her! Look at her!'

The sister was walking unsteadily around gripping her own crotch. She looked very small in the shot, almost dwarfish, but it may have been the camera angle. The wife kicked her husband and kneed him, and head butted him, knowing that he wouldn't retaliate in the presence of the doormen. She was trying to get him to hit her, so that everyone would see what kind of a man he really was. I found this film embarrassing, but the rest of the audience was creased up with laughter. There, also captured on the video, was the audience witnessing the original scene, huddled in the doorway of the club. They were clearly enjoying the spectacle of raw passion unfolding in front of them.

This film went on forever. The violence was episodic. Every now and then one or other of the protagonists would disappear down the steps away from the club, and the remaining one would sidle up to the door and attempt to persuade the bouncers that they were not at fault. They would try to do this as calmly and as rationally as possible. Neither wanted to be the one that was barred from the club. In the middle of all that violence and screaming and blood and pain, that's what they were most concerned with.

But they were both barred in the end. They didn't just get a knock-back, they were both barred.

It was funny really, they never talked about the real backgrounds of the individuals caught in the security cameras. They never discussed the state of their marriages, their financial problems, the effects of redundancy on them. How could they? They didn't know them.

One day they would be nameless ordinary punters, who queued up and paid to get in, the next they would have a name of sorts, the video title, and they would be barred. They never saw them again, except when they came to the door to get their knock-back. They had no real history, as far as they were concerned.

I told everybody that I needed some air. The air was almost clear at that time of the morning. Presumably, it would have been a lot dirtier when the steel mills were still going. The birds were singing outside the town hall, long before the dawn. I wasn't sure whether pigeons sang like that or not. I had never seen anything else in the centre of Sheffield.

There was a fading poster saying 'Support the Miners'. Someone had written 'before it's too late' across the bottom of it. I got a pen out of my coat and wrote something for myself. 'It's already too late', I scribbled in black right across it. I was giggling like a child. It was a funny sort of laughter, half-sad and half-happy.

I thought of my brother and the North he had talked about. This wasn't it, I knew that. He had been driven here by his idealism and he had somehow managed to find the very heart of the North and strength in class solidarity in this very same place. This very same place.

I looked out at the empty streets, my eyes stinging because of the smoke in the club. I had been distracted somewhere along the way and ended up in this sub-culture of Thatcherite values, where dog was eating dog right before my very eyes and the only goal seemed to be to climb on the shoulder of one's neighbours to stand above them for just a few moments. To be a somebody with what was left.

Jumping the queue so that the punters in the rain would say 'Who's that?' Staying behind in the club after hours as the mug punters filed out. Watching the videos of the punters fighting each other or trying to fight one of the bouncers, and giving us all a good laugh in the process.

He hadn't seen this side of things. It was just my misfortune I suppose that things were changing. The North was changing. I wished that he was here with me to show me the way. I was that lost.

I walked slowly back to the club and pressed the buzzer to get in. Becksy came to the door. 'Back again?' he said puzzled to see me. 'Can't you wait for tomorrow night?'

They were still watching videos. I waited patiently for the second film to end, and the laughter to cease finally. And this small crowd of desperate spectators to disperse. It was Fat Eddie I needed to talk to. On his own.

He sat there, hunched over his drink. Red, bleary eyes. Waiting for a refill. He was surprised to see me back.

There were no preliminaries. No chit chat, no comments on the action in the video, no cracks about how lucky we were to be allowed to stay there until this time of the morning. None of that.

'Where does Adele really work?' I asked. 'Please.'

The video was still on above his head, and it lit up his face, which looked loose and pasty close up. He looked at me, almost as if he felt sorry for me. It was the 'please' I suppose. I was begging and he knew it.

'Hasn't she talked about it with you?' he said, slurring his words. I shook my head.

'The lads and I were wondering if you knew,' he said.

'Some blokes don't like it. Some blokes get a fucking kick out of it. I know which way I fall.' And he looked at me again, and winked. 'I know what side I hang on.'

I didn't respond.

'And you know nothing about it?' he asked.

I shook my head again, preparing myself. 'Didn't Lenny ever tell you? You know Big Lenny, don't you?'

I told him that I hadn't ever mentioned Adele to Lenny. Adele and I together had avoided his club.

I knew what was coming from that moment. If I could have, I would have left there and then. I didn't want to hear the words themselves.

'She's on the game,' he said, almost with a shrug which said 'no big deal'. 'It's a decent sort of place, mind you. In fact, a friend of mine owns it. It's very clean. And don't worry, she uses condoms. They have to there. My pal is very strict about that. No bare back riding in that joint.'

I looked away. The screen was filled with more pain. Somebody had put another tape on. I was wondering if somebody might be filming me standing there, just for a nobble, to be watched for a laugh one day.

'I've fucked her,' said Big Eddie almost eagerly. 'In her professional capacity, of course,' he said.

I thanked him inaudibly, and signaled that I had heard enough as I started to walk off towards the gold hand rail to take me away from the VIP area. I couldn't really speak; I was choked with emotion.

'And socially,' said Fat Eddie as I started slowly walking away. 'And the truth is,' he shouted after me, 'I don't know which was fucking better.'

And his laughter echoed around the empty club and followed me out onto the grey, wet street.

# FIFTEEN

A taxi took me to Adele's flat that night. She had never taken me there. There was always some good reason.

She often said that there was a jealous boyfriend from before who liked to threaten anybody she was seeing. He liked to hang about, outside, she said, he was threatening and very violent. She was always very vague about every aspect of this former boyfriend, except his threatening and violent nature.

But I remembered the address from that night in the casino. I took a taxi and sat crumpled up like a foetus in her front garden, just waiting. I didn't have to wait that long. It was nearly half four in the morning when I saw a green Jag drive up. It had personalized plates - 'M2 ME'. I didn't feel like laughing at this pathetic attempt to claim individuality through financial and imaginative enterprise.

I could see her sitting in the front with some large menacing looking man with a squarish head and a double chin bulging out of his tight collar. They were laughing together. He was smoking and blowing the smoke out his side window. He was gesturing with a cigarette in his hand. It sounded like some story or other. The story finished with her falling back laughing even louder. He put his arm around her shoulder heaving with mirth.

Then he said something to her. I couldn't make out the words but through the open window I could make out the rising pattern of a question. Or a request. That distinctive rise. There was no pleading or repetition in the request. It was just a matter of fact sort of question. Then she started to bend forward until her head moved down out of my sight. It stayed there. I felt sick as the seconds grew. My queasiness might have been due to the taste of the metallic lager in my mouth, or the fights on the video that I had been witnessing, or the lateness of the hour, but I know that it was none of these things. I could feel my body start to tremble uncontrollably, all by itself without any volition, and I looked away.

When I glanced back she was starting to sit up and wiping her mouth with a tissue. He was handing her another one, as if he had several nice and convenient. As if this was all something to be expected. They were still laughing as she got out of the car. He tooted and drove off. She waved after him. She looked as if she didn't have a care in the world.

I hid behind the side wall of the house, and waited until I heard the clunk of the key in the door before I approached her. She looked shocked to see me.

'Hiya,' she said. The greeting, if that's what it was, came out stretched and rising like a question.

'How did you find out where my place was?' she asked.

'It wasn't hard,' I said. I was sounding like Big Lenny, like a man who knew things. 'Have you just got here?' she asked. I could see that look in her eyes, the pupils getting bigger to take in all the details and nuances of life, like a survival mechanism.

I nodded. 'I was round the back of the flats just seeing if there was a light on in your flat,' I said. 'I wasn't going to disturb you if you were already asleep.' I sounded in control, even though inside I was in turmoil.

Freud had once written something like 'He that has eyes to see and ears to hear may convince himself that no mortal can keep a secret. If his lips are silent, he chatters with his finger-tips; betrayal oozes out of him at every pore.' But Freud wasn't right even here. Not even here. I wasn't chattering with my finger-tips. My feelings were not revealed.

She opened that front door for me and I walked in slowly and carefully just behind her with all of my emotions in control, never betraying, even for an instant, how I really felt. I breathed in deeply and audibly. Like a sigh. When we got inside the flat I knew that everything Fat Eddie had told me about her was right. This was not the flat of a nurse or a beautician. I could see all of the expensive evidence tossed so carefully around me.

She gestured for me to sit down, but I stood where I was in the middle of the floor. She stood facing me, well not facing me, her face was nowhere to be seen, it was pointing downwards at an angle. But she was watching me carefully. Her long manicured fingers, with traces of body oils still no doubt on them, moving repetitively across the back of her other hand. She was on her guard.

'Did you get a taxi home?' I asked. My voice was starting to crack. I knew it, and she could sense it. I could see a flicker in her eyes. An almost incessant blinking, which she was fighting to control, to keep her eyes wide and beautiful and innocent at that time of the morning after a night of smoke, and the stress of expectation, and sex. I could see the anxiety in her face even at that angle.

'My boss gave me a lift home tonight actually,' she said. It came out as a single tone group, as fluent as you like. Unbroken by hesitation or breath pause. She was watching me for some sign. I could sense the fear within her. I could almost smell the fear even above that overpowering smell of sex, dosed with the most expensive perfumes she could afford. I could smell the freshmint. She was always studiously clean. But nothing could hide those primitive smells of sex and fear at that moment. Nothing.

'I saw you,' I said. I tried to smile openly as if to indicate to her that there was no point in denying it. A gay open smile, a little carefree perhaps. It must have looked quite bizarre at that precise moment in time. 'Really?' she replied. Her body was in a tight, closed posture with her eyebrows knitted across her face, guarding that delicate region.

'I saw what you were doing,' I said calmly.

'And what was that?' she asked nonchalantly, without changing position or posture.

'I saw it all,' I said.

'Oh, you mean when I dropped something in his car?' she replied. 'Is that what you saw?' She tried to make an unconcerned expression but it wavered there in front of me, as if it knew that it didn't belong there at that time. As if it didn't know what it had been brought out for, as if it didn't know what it was to do next. Then it settled on her face, as she took control of it; the expression itself smug, confident, cock-sure, practiced. It said a lot about her, and a lot about what she thought of me.

Nothing.

It was that expression that did it. My hand swung out instinctively, violently, before I could take control. I was almost weeping before it landed. At least, my eyes were closed so I never saw what it did.

I never witnessed it.

# SIXTEEN

Neither of us slept in what remained of that night. We lay side by side on her bed for a few hours in her darkened bedroom, with her thick curtains keeping out the creeping, prowling dawn with all its nasty little secrets to reveal.

'We need to talk,' she said. 'And not about me. You already know all about me. I assume. Let me tell you about your brother,' she said.

'I'd had enough of men in this town, and then I met Phil,' she said. 'He was different. That's all I can say. He was different.' I nodded my head without looking at her. 'He told me all about his work at Cambridge for his psychology degree.' She was smiling. 'That's right Cambridge.'

I made a small snorting noise, as if to say that I couldn't bear to hear any more of her lies. But after what had happened, I knew that the time for lies had gone.

'I didn't know then that it was all just made up until that first night with you,' she said. 'I can laugh about it now.'

I had to look her way to get her to continue. It was a painful sight. 'The truth is', she continued. 'I used to love him analyzing me. He was so good at telling me what I was thinking and what I was feeling. Don't ask me how he did it. He was a really good psychologist.'

I found myself nodding empathetically.

'Even though,' she added. 'I suppose that he picked most of it up from you. He didn't actually go to Cambridge, isn't that right?'

I sat there trying to imagine my brother saying such false things in this room. I looked around the room, and tried to imagine these words filling the fragrant air.

'You see,' she began, 'I was always worried about how your mother would react to me. You being from such a posh family and all that. Phil told me all about your big house and your dad who was the famous academic. I don't come from that type of family background at all. You see I left home when I was sixteen. I got booted out. I've had to work to get by. Phil said that he understood, but not everybody is as open-minded as your brother.'

I didn't have the strength to tell her that this had been lies too. I had not talked to her about *my* ... about *our* background. I'm not sure why.

Then she slowly started to tell me all about what my brother had told her about Cambridge and my lecturer with the brown tweed jacket using his pompous alliteration to talk about the predictive power of proper science. I heard all about my own undergraduate room in Cambridge and the print of the young Chatterton on the wall opposite the window seat. I even heard details of the very first practical I had ever done in psychology and the mark I got for it. I heard about the significance of iconic gestures and the importance of eye gaze as windows to the human soul. These all sounded better somehow even in that room in the dawn, having been dressed up by my brother. It all sounded so glamorous down there by the Cam. The May Balls, the punt on the river, the scientific breakthroughs on the microscopic analyses of human behaviour. The certainty of it all. The career trajectory. She had been enthralled with him, and he had borrowed bits of my life to keep her enthralled.

'I didn't realize it was all just a story,' she said. 'He was no different to the rest of them around here. Then there was you. The shy younger brother. But I saw a bit of him in you. And the stories were the same. I was hearing some of them for the second time. It was like meeting him all over again.'

She was laughing now and the laughter was causing her to flinch with the physical pain in her tightened face. 'I didn't mean to hurt you. We shouldn't have got to know each other,' she said. 'We were never right for each other. I just wanted to be remind-ed of him. I'm sorry.'

I was crying. Maybe it was shame, maybe it was sorrow. She reached out her hand, but I pushed it away.

'Phil always knew what I did,' she said. 'Right from the start. That's how we met. He and a friend turned up one night at the sauna where I work, after they'd been to a club. The thought that he was getting for free what other men had to pay for turned him on, I think.'

I sat there in silence, trying to take this all in.

'Tell me about Phil at Orgreave?' I said. 'Tell me about that.' I wanted to remember something positive about him. I needed something.

'Orgreave?' she said.

'Yes, Orgreave.'

'He wasn't at Orgreave,' she said. 'He was in bed with me the day of the really big battle. He had moved in with me at that time. I was looking after him.' She was looking at me carefully. 'I was keeping him, in fact. My cousin was there. Perhaps you're just getting a bit mixed-up. My cousin was a miner. He was on strike then.'

'I don't understand,' I said.

'You're just a bit confused,' she said. 'My cousin used to bring some of the food parcels up here for me and Phil. He couldn't eat them all himself. He said that all these food parcels came from comrades in Russia and Poland, but they were all local brands. Heinz Baked Beans, tins of skimmed milk, packets of tea bags and tins of stewed meat. But even my cousin Brian didn't stay out of work that long. He got a job on the door of a club for most of the strike. I got him fixed up with that. He was getting twelve quid a night. I know that. Brian was at Orgreave. Not Phil.'

I sat there not speaking.

'I remember that,' she continued, 'because Brian lost one of his slip-ons when he ran from the police at Orgreave, and he wanted me to go back there to look for it with him the next day. Phil and I were in bed together when he was telling us all about it. Phil was creased up with laughter hearing Brian's stories about the miners facing up to the police. He said that they were all fucking nutcases. Phil was too sensible to go anywhere like Orgreave.'

I sat there and she held my hand and said again that she was sorry. I didn't know what to say.

'I'll not be working tonight,' she said. 'My boss will kill me if I turn up like this. You've got a date tonight, if you want one,' she said, and pulled me close. 'If you want it?'

# SEVENTEEN

I watched the video-recording of the incident in the club many times, after I watched it with Lenny. I was still seeing Adele, and for the first time I felt this need in her.

It was me who had become cold. Perhaps, my brother was right after all. About something. Even Nila commented that I had changed. She did not like the person that I was becoming. This harder soul.

I had seen the worst parts of the video-recording of the murder, and I knew that I could sit through it on my own. I knew where to stop the recording in order to miss the killing itself. I had written the time of the killing down in pencil on a scrap of paper in that darkened room and I had underlined it. I was only interested in what happened before that point. I still had my work to do.

My anxiety about the tape was that without the transcripts of the speech I was in danger of making the kinds of errors that Cliff and others make when they view behaviour. For a while, I contemplated saying that there was nothing in the video for me to comment on. But I knew inside that I had to say something significant now, after I had heard about Phil's deceptions on top of all the other deceptions that I had been running into ever since I had come to Sheffield. I was a psychologist, and not just another punter trying to get by with just fancy words and stories and fragments of other people's lives.

I had to see something in the tape and in the flux of behaviour. Something that Cliff and Big Lenny and my brother couldn't possibly see. Something which would tell others and tell myself who I really was.

I played the video-tape over and over again in that darkened room, trying to put Lenny's words out of my mind. I watched the three men enter the bar. I timed their entrance, and measured how far they sat from the other couple. Distance, time, speed, every small thing could be significant here. I didn't want to miss anything out.

I watched the girl in the sexy dress display her tell-tale look. Well, not so tell-tale a look any longer. It was a glance. Nothing more, nothing less. A glance around the room without making eye contact at any specific individual. There was nothing to read into it, except Lenny's premature interpretation. I wrote down 'room-encompassing look displayed at this point. Not significant to the structure of the subsequent interaction.'

I watched the three men display their 'sly' looks at each other. That was Lenny's word as well. These were slippery concepts he used. Lenny lived in a world of sly looks and women with guilt written all over their faces. A world of devious and dubious meaning in the behaviour, before the behaviour itself was even described. A world which was understood at a glance.

The guy in the leather jacket's face did show significant changes though. I isolated the individual frames of the video-recordings of the facial movements one by one.

I scored the frowning upper brow movement, the raised upper lid of the eye, the wrinkled lower lid, the dilated nostrils, the open lips, the lower teeth exposed and the depressed lower lip movement on the face of the man in the leather jacket, and charted carefully their changes this way and that. That was a recognizable emotional configuration. I could put a name to it. It was anger.

Then I started to describe all this microscopic and fleeting action in that face in much greater detail. The kind of details that we, psychologists, need to work with – the technical details. I watched him raise the upper lid, and scored how the centre of the upper lip was drawn straight up whilst the outer portions of the upper lip were drawn up but not as high as the centre, causing an angular bend in the shape of the upper lip. I watched him raise the infra orbital triangle causing the infra orbital furrow to deepen. I scored how this deepens the nasolabial furrows and raises the upper part of this furrow. I watched him widen and raise the nostril wings causing the lips to part.

Sometimes we think we take it all in, as behaviour dances across our view, but believe me we miss most of what is happening out there. I could see all of this in front of me for the first time. I sat long into the night scoring three crucial seconds of film.

The confrontation between the two was really an emotional dance of sorts. A reaction to microscopic movements in each other, involving the muscular apparatus of the human face, one of the most sophisticated signalling systems in the world. I saw anger there. I saw some surprise, and a little fear at times. At least I did in the case of the man in the leather jacket. The perpetrator of the violence. But in the case of the victim I saw only minimal emotion, the rest all dampened down by that great mask of a smile that hung there throughout, and presumably the effects of all that alcohol.

Then there was the posture. It was certainly a significant configuration of seated postures of the three men who had arrived together. Two were in exactly the same posture as each other, in postural echo. They had their arms folded, their legs tucked under the counter of the bar, their heads slightly rotated. The victim was in quite a different posture to them. He was oriented exclusively towards the blonde in the sexy dress. Could this posture be construed as aggressive? Not without a detailed understanding of the sub-culture in which they were operating, in which a man may have certain proprietorial rights over a woman. And not without a detailed understanding of what might count as a violation of such rights.

I looked at the final frames of facial expression of the man in the leather jacket. The imminent action of this dangerous man seemed to be signaled through the immobility of his expression. The man in the grey suit smiled back at him, a wavering sideways smile. Was this where the aggressiveness slipped in? An inappropriate reaction to a deadly threat? Perhaps he just didn't see it. Perhaps we needed the benefit of hindsight to see it.

Then there was that eye contact. Two men looking at each other for perhaps a full minute. No words exchanged, mutual gaze culminating in one man trembling or shaking. This was just too ambiguous. And then the touch preceded by that small but very significant gesture. The gesture where his right hand stretched out, then started to make a claw and then eventually a fist. Two fingers together dragging the others behind. Then the same hand settled on the back of the girl in the leather dress and moved slowly in a gentle smooth arc down the back of her shiny leather dress. You could see the disbelief on the man in the leather jacket's face clearly from the video. These frames were amongst the most obvious. So was that the aggressive act on the part of the man about to be killed?

I thought of Cliff and imagined what he would say. 'Provocative, yes,' he would say. 'Very provocative.' I could even hear him saying it. Even John back in Cambridge sprang to mind. The freezing necessity of touch. That was surely the significant element in that whole incident in that after-hours drinking den. And what about the gesture that preceded it. It was an iconic gesture, but what was it representing here? The whole thrust of my research was that the gesture acts with the speech to form a single cognitive representation. But we didn't have any transcripts. Without the speech, we just had a small claw like gesture moving forward in space. The fingers making a claw then a fist. A fist.

That could be perceived as very threatening. A fist followed by a provocative touch.

I wrote my report thinking of Cliff and the machinations of the law. There was evidence of threatening and aggressive provocation on the victim's part. Threatening and aggressive provocation. These were the very words I used. I delivered my report to my professor by hand. I watched him read it carefully and deliberately. I watched his eye-movements track across the page and the beginnings of a smile start in the corners of his lips. My professor coughed politely when he had finished and then turned to me and said that he was very pleased with the content of the report. Very pleased indeed.

'Good man,' he said, and then he repeated it once more without even looking at me. I knew that Cambridge would never let me down. And he patted me on the back in a patronizing sort of way, although, of course, he wouldn't have seen it like this.

I was just pleased that something was going right in my life.

# EIGHTEEN

One afternoon out of the blue, Lenny and five of his firm arrived at the department. I was out when they called. When I got back, I noticed that Stanley the porter had made them all a cup of tea. He never did it for anybody else. They were all sitting behind the glass partition, with their feet up, talking about the good old days in the steel mills. They had something in common and I envied them.

'Fucking skiving again,' said Lenny, when I arrived. 'I told the lads all about your lab and they all wanted to come up here for a nosey around. We were just passing.'

I asked Lenny what he really had in mind, as they all followed me in silence towards my office. He said that he was interested in nonverbal leakage for selection purposes for some work opportunities. Big Lenny said that he would act as an experimenter with me. 'I've already been done, lads, you see,' he said. 'It's your turn now with the doc.'

Big Lenny told me to load the slides into the carousel and that he would strap them one by one into the chair. They all stood in an arc around the chair, wondering who might go first.

'This doesn't involve any electric shocks?' asked Steve. 'Because my doctor has told me that I've got an irregular heartbeat. An electric current could send it shooting all over the place.'

'Sit down and shut the fuck up,' said Big Lenny. 'You can go first now. You've just selected yourself. That's part of the test and you've just fucked it up.' Big Lenny told the rest to go and wait in the waiting room. 'And no smoking,' he warned. 'That might interfere with the results.'

Steve was strapped into the chair. The straps weren't really necessary. They were there for another experiment, but Big Lenny insisted on them. Steve sat there quietly, looking very anxious as Big Lenny attached the electrodes for the galvanic skin response. Steve was sweating slightly and the experiment hadn't yet begun.

'Listen,' he said to me. He was almost pleading. 'I'm not kidding about this heartbeat of mine. I'm putting my life in your hands here, doc.'

'He's a professional,' said Big Lenny to Steve. 'Do you think that he brings people here and fucking kills them? Relax for fuck's sake. I've done it already. It's nothing.'

'You see,' said Big Lenny to me behind Steve's back, 'I think that this research of yours is very interesting. It was spot on with me.'

'Just relax,' he said to Steve. 'Listen,' said Steve, 'if I get one shock I'm getting up and leaving. Do you both understand that? I'm not here to have a load of electricity put through me.'

'Okay,' I said, 'I'm going to show you a series of photographs, Steve, and I'm just going to measure your skin response to them, that's all. Big Lenny and I will leave the room and the photographs will come on automatically. Do you understand that?'

'Okay, doc,' he said. 'I trust you. I'm game for it. You're not going to fuck me about, I know that.'

Big Lenny had started to walk off. 'Oh by the way, doc,' Steve said to me. He was sounding like a condemned man trying to extend his last few minutes on this earth. 'Adele is your bird, right? Well I've heard that she talks about you all the time. She's fallen for you big style. That's all. Big Style.'

I could feel my own heart racing at that point. I felt like a man who had been under siege with a first hint that the enemy might now be leaving the gates of the city. A man whose defenses might be able to come down at last.

Big Lenny and I went into the control room, and watched Steve through the one-way mirror sitting there sweating, looking anxious. The first photograph burst into life in front of him. I watched his face for signs of micro-expressions. He looked so anxious to begin with that few of the photographs seemed to disrupt his look at all.

'You know,' said Big Lenny. 'I don't think that these photographs are strong enough for lads of this calibre. I've got a little experiment all of my own planned for today.'

He reached into his jacket pocket and pulled a black balaclava out of one pocket and a long wide blade in a leather case out of the other.

'Keep filming, doc,' he said, as he handed me the leather sheath. I was so surprised that I couldn't really say anything. I watched Big Lenny creep to the door and then spring into the room right in front of Steve sitting in that chair with the electrodes on his hand, waiting for the electric current to come. Big Lenny thrust the knife right forward until I could hear cloth tearing.

'Fuck,' shouted Steve, trying to get free of the straps. Big Lenny pulled the balaclava off. He was howling with laughter. 'I hope that you've got all that on film, doc,' said Big Lenny. 'I want you to analyze his behaviour and tell me how much control he would have in an emergency situation. Has he crapped himself or what?'

When the two of them came into the control room I was quite pale, in fact nearly as pale as Steve himself. Then Big Lenny went to the waiting room and led the rest of his firm one-by-one to the experimental room. He made the same entrance more or less with the flashing blade with each of his men in turn, and afterwards he and I went through the video. I was looking for the tell-tale signs of surprise and fear. The raised brows, the raised upper lids, the open lips. I was documenting the changes in the major muscle groups. He was looking for something slightly more global. He wanted three from the five selected on the basis of this analysis. He was laughing loudly at all their reactions. We both did our ordering separately. We disagreed on only one - Steve himself. I said that he should be in on the work opportunity, Big Lenny said that he should be out. But he was persuaded in the end.

'You're the fucking expert,' he said. 'Even though I swear that he nearly shat himself when I came in with the knife.'

I didn't really disagree with Lenny, but I felt that I owed Steve one for what he had told me about Adele. I got Steve in on whatever big lucrative job was going.

'Oh by the way,' said Lenny, as he was leaving. 'Is it true that you're seeing Adele?'

'Adele who?' I asked. 'Don't be funny with me, cunt,' he said. 'There is only one Adele I know of. Anyway, listen, I'm not bothered about what she does for a living.' I went to say 'please don't say any more', but he just stopped me with a short sharp openhanded gesture. 'Or,' he continued, 'whether you live off her. I don't give a fuck about that either. In my opinion all women are fucking whores anyway. If you want a fuck you take them out for a meal or you buy them a drink. A half a lager, if you're lucky. It's all the same. It's all money changing hands, one way or another. But I don't know if you know who she works for. Mick Eccles is a bad 'un. Keep out of his way.'

'I hear ...' Then he corrected himself. 'I know for a fact that he has the girls who work for him do drug runs for him. They carry the gear for him. Keep out of that guy's way for fuck's sake. Okay?'

'Of course,' I said. 'I'm not stupid.'

'Make sure that you're not. And thanks for today, doc,' he said. 'Fucking marvelous.' And he shook my hand warmly for the very first time since I had known him.

# NINETEEN

It was about a month later. I had nearly forgotten all about that afternoon with Lenny and Steve and the boys, when Adele came back from work one Friday afternoon and suddenly announced that we were going on a surprise trip.

'All booked up and ready to go,' she said. The trip was to Amsterdam.

I had never been before, but Adele told me that she had been just the once. 'It's not sleazy really,' she said. 'You'll love it.' We got a taxi to Manchester airport, and I witnessed this girly excitement in her face. We arrived at Schiphol airport in the afternoon and she pointed at the cigarette machine saying 'SHAG' in bright red letters. She was like a child.

'It just means tobacco,' she said. 'Isn't that a right gas?'

We took a taxi to our hotel by a park, and we walked arm in arm though the children and the roller bladers in the early summer sun. She was happy and contented. It was just a weekend together, a weekend that flew past in a succession of new images and sounds and smells. The porn in the windows next to the shopping arcade. The women sitting in the windows, bathed in mellow red light, smoking and waiting.

Adele just pointed out how normal and attractive they were. 'Just normal girls,' she said. 'Just normal girls, like me.'

I didn't, of course, feel comfortable with what she did, but I was learning to control my thoughts and my actions. I had to. I had learned that. Sometimes, I felt a terrible guilt about seeing my brother's girlfriend, especially now that I knew that she had really loved him. But I controlled that too. Perhaps, I had needed all of this. Perhaps I needed to break away from my privileged past, and experience some of the pain and the hurt of the world. Perhaps, my brother had done me the greatest favour of all, he had taken me here and arranged this whole situation for me. He had even pretended that he was me, to take away the paper qualifications that I had become used to waving around. To be somebody. He had done all this, so that the real me would have to emerge without the assistance of all of those props like Frank's roller or the personalized number plate of Adele's boss. The real me.

Whoever that might be.

The outside world for once seemed a long way off. And then on the last night just before we left the hotel, the phone in our room went, like a shrill warning of imminent danger. I didn't know that anybody knew we were there. Adele answered the phone. My colour drained away.

She talked quietly down the phone. I couldn't hear what she was saying, but I watched her talk. I watched her edgy incomplete gestures. It was something that was making her anxious, but she never said anything other than 'yeah', 'yeah' and 'sure' down that treacherous, deceptive little line.

As soon as she turned to me I knew that Freud had been right about something after all. Her betrayal oozed out of her. I had always thought that this was a strange choice of word for that Austrian gentleman, until that night. Body juices ooze out of insects, sores ooze pus. It is not a nice word.

She said that a friend had managed to leave a suitcase behind her in Amsterdam and that she had just rung to ask Adele to bring the case back to England with her. The suitcase was to be delivered to our hotel within the next half hour. We sat together and we didn't talk. I didn't want to hear any of her lies.

'I'm tired,' I said. 'It's because we've had such a good time.' Adele spent a lot of time putting her make-up on in the bathroom. It kept her busy, I suppose.

On the way to the airport Adele quite suddenly asked me to carry the new case. It was a question performed without even looking at me, except for the briefest of glances. But there was a gesture alright. A little flick of the right hand which transferred the case from her to me.

'Get shot of them,' Lenny had always said about troublemakers in his club. 'Get fucking shot of them.' It reminded me of that. And that's what she was signifying with that little gesture. So quietly, and so deceptively.

'It's really heavy,' she said, continuing unnecessarily. 'Could you carry it? You've only got an overnight bag with you. I've got this big case already with all my clothes and make-up in it.'

I said that I would carry the case and that it was no problem, and I carried this heavy black case all the way from the taxi to the check-in.

'Thank you,' she said, and she kissed me warm and deep as we sat down together on the plane, holding hands but I felt the warmth of the touch turn slowly into fear and loathing. Until a touch became almost impossible.

When we got to Manchester airport her bag came first, and she said that she would go through Customs quickly to get a taxi ready for us.

'Good idea,' I said.

I watched her first few steps away and I felt the deepest of sadnesses inside. The sadness of being left behind again, the sadness of my brother's walk, the sadness of another world at an end.

My bag came eventually and I walked through the 'Nothing to declare' channel with my heart pounding, after her. They stopped me. I saw her glance behind her and then walk on quickly. I don't know why they stopped me. They may have heard that drum beat in my chest. My colour might have left me. I don't know. But he suddenly emerged from behind a one-way mirror and motioned for me to stop. He knew nothing about me, or my weekend devoured by a final lust with my brother's lover. But he knew enough to stop me there and then. He asked me to open my bag, he was watching my face and monitoring every leaking micro-expression that flitted before him, and I did so carefully and cautiously.

My small overnight bag, that is. The black case, with the tags ripped off, had been left in a cubicle in the men's toilet at Manchester airport several minutes before.

# TWENTY

She didn't wait for me. This was just more confirmation. I got home late on my own and went straight to bed. I wanted sleep to end this particular episode but there was a storm that night. I started to drift off to sleep and the rain began to sound like a fire crackling. I know that this is an unlikely image, but that's how it sounded. Like a fire just outside my window. Threatening and irregular enough to keep me awake. I woke up late and bleary-eyed.

I kept the curtains closed for as long as I could, so that I could hide in that half-dark world. I felt sick inside. It was an empty sort of nausea. I had always believed that different emotions were based on the same basic physiological changes in the body and how you felt was really to do with attribution and interpretation. The mind in other words, rational and probing and trying to work out the reasons why things were as they were. Anger and euphoria both derivable from the same basic discharges of the autonomic nervous system. But I was wrong. I was sick with fear. There was no other emotion to feel from the jingle jangle of the neuronal impulses careering though my body. Just fear. Sick with fear of that man with the large square head.

Girlfriend. That's a joke. That's some terrible joke. Some tart who fell for my brother, a tart who was the biggest liar in England. No worse. A tart who fell for my brother who pretended to be me. I laughed a short sharp laugh before the nausea returned. I stayed there all afternoon and into the evening, forming plans and strategies in my head that ran their course to depressing and sometimes frightening conclusions. I could see the lads starting to congregate on the corner and I sat there wishing that they were still my only problem.

The phone went with a shrill ring and I jumped, but I stayed where I was. Like some poor fucking animal that was too terrified to move. The landlady called up for me, but by the time that I got down the caller had gone. It was Adele. My landlady had recognized her voice immediately and had tried to talk to her but she pretended to be somebody else. So much for her impersonations, so much for her acting in the massage parlour in the afternoons with tired old men blowing their redundancy money on a few short, sharp shuffles of the hand.

She was just checking with her phone call. They knew that I had not been arrested and detained but they didn't know why. Her boss must have assumed that I had talked, he guessed that I had sung like a fucking canary and that he was in the process of being set up. He rang that night very late. It was a voice that I didn't recognize but it was strangely familiar. Those South Yorkshire vowels cut to nothing. The voice said just two things 'I want my fucking gear' and 'you're fucking dead'. There was a noticeable pause between these two things and a long pause afterwards before he hung up. I could hear him and me breathing in that same quiet space. His message left me wondering for many hours. If I somehow managed to retrieve the gear was I dead anyway? I thought that it was a curiously illogical sort of message. But I suppose that if I am being truthful the lack of logic frightened me most of all. I was not used to reasoning with people who cared little for the logical connectives of everyday talk or everyday life, the connectives that bind rational thought together.

I rang my mother and tried to tell her that I had got into some sort of trouble, but she didn't want to listen to me. She just said that I was always trouble, ever since I was a boy. I was an odd sort of child, odd and peculiar as far back as she could remember and always a cause of heartache. Even worse since I had become that know-all at university who looked down his nose at everyone else in the family. 'Why couldn't you be more like your brother?' she asked. 'Why?' She was sobbing in a drunken sort of self-pitying way in the middle of the afternoon. She was no help at all. Worse than no help, she made me feel isolated, alone and angry. More like my brother, that was a laugh. The so-called Cambridge student who claimed to have spent lonely years watching behaviour through dusty one-way mirrors. The man who had got me into all of this through Adele and the man with the square head and his weekend runs to Amsterdam. More like my brother indeed.

I slipped out of the house the next afternoon and took an unfamiliar route to get some groceries, past the butchers with the glistening chunks of thick butchered meat on hooks in the window, past strangers with eyes that looked sly and devious and moved after me, past a policeman who followed my tracking gaze, past children with shrill piercing voices in the afternoon. I felt afraid and distracted, aware of all the danger out there. Danger that need never be signaled, intentions that can never be read. I went back to my bedsit and sat in stillness, all the time thinking of what I could do and who I could go to. I worked my way through all the people who could possibly, just possibly help me, but I was sure that they would all let me down one by one, these cardboard figures of my imagination falling as I walked up to them to ask for some sort of help. The wind was still tapping on my window like some tired old man wanting in, wanting my attention distracting me when my thoughts almost, almost reached a conclusion.

I had plans in abundance, the plans of a trained observer. I knew something of this man's behaviour and habits. He liked screwing the girls who worked for him, especially the young fresh ones. I was going to find the newest girl who worked for him. That was going to be easy. Then I was going to take my mother's advice and become more like my brother. In fact, I was going to become him. Charismatic and charming and full of easy-going lies and deceit and make this girl, this new girl full of enthusiasm and as gullible as fuck, fall in love with me. Then I was going to give this girl something for him, a parcel, a present, something good. Then I was going to ring the police and have this bastard busted for possession of this kilo of hash or jam jar full of heroin or whatever. It was an elegant sort of plan, full of the logically connected propositions that the mind seems to like when it is working like mine at this moment in time, full of urgency darting this way and that on a curious journey all of its own making.

Late that afternoon there was a knock on the front door of the house. It was a loud insistent knock. I knew that they had come for me. Nobody normal knocked like that. Somebody from downstairs let him in. I heard the heavy boots on the creaky stairs, and then the same heavy knock on my own door. I sat up in bed immediately, quite naked, with the bedspread around me. Whoever it was knocked again and then flung the door wide open causing paint chippings to scatter off the wall behind the door.

I jumped out of bed to grab my pants hanging over the arm-chair, but it was too late. He was in the room. Standing there, grinning, that big lop-sided grin on that massive head of his. It was Lenny. He was laughing. 'You fucking student,' he said, 'don't you ever do anything apart from lie in bed?' He always wore that expression when he knew something that you didn't. 'What do you know?' he always liked to ask when he was out and about. I should have asked him what he knew at that precise moment because he looked so pleased with himself that he obviously knew something.

He sat down on one corner of the bed, he said that he had some important news, and he told me to sit down. I was covering myself with my jeans held out in front of me. He pointed down at them and laughed. 'I hope that you've got something on down there,' he said. 'I don't want any nasty surprises.'

I had never seen him dressed casually before and all I remember thinking was how normal he looked dressed like that with a sweatshirt and jeans and a shaving rash quite visible in the cold light of my room. He asked me how I had been and when I said 'fine', he laughed again.

'Really?' he said.

'Yeah really,' I replied. I assumed that he had come round to witness my suffering first hand. Then he came out with it, but not at first. He liked a slow build up. He told me that he had heard that Mick, Adele's boss, was having a bit of trouble with somebody. Somebody who had been to Amsterdam recently. His head sort of nodded in my direction as if he was hitting a football my way. 'Do you know anybody who's been over to Amsterdam lately? Any wanker that is?'

'Well,' he began, 'they've all been having a laugh about it down in the club. Apparently, this dodgy bird gives this wanker some white powder to take through customs. Does any of this sound familiar?' he asked.

'Not really,' I said.

'Anyway,' he continued, leaning back on that part of the bed he was occupying, stretching those big horny hands out behind him. 'Anyway,' he repeated, 'this bird gives him some white powder to carry through customs alright, some white … fucking talcum powder that is.' And I watched Lenny explode into laughter with his spit flying everywhere. He could hardly speak with all that laughing.

'You dumped a load of talcum powder in the airport,' said Lenny. 'You like to live dangerously alright. You let birds put a load of talcum powder into your bag and then you go and dump it all.'

'You see,' Lenny continued, 'Mick was worried that Adele was getting too, how can I put this … a little too keen on somebody.

So he wanted to see if she would set him up if he asked her to do it. And she did.' He was still laughing. 'That's what you meant to her. Absolutely nothing. Absolutely sweet FA.'

I grunted, but didn't speak.

'You know what they say about fucking whores,' said Lenny. 'Even Mick says that, and he's married to one. He's got a kid with one of them for fuck's sake and he still says it.'

'Then Mick rings you up and fucking threatens you,' said Lenny. 'He's testing your response. He records the whole thing with this little tape recorder that he's got with a mike that sticks on the backs of the handsets and then he plays the tape when he's out and about, for a bit of a nobble. You want to hear the way that you are breathing on that fucking tape. Everyone pisses themselves fucking laughing when they hear it. They can all tell that you're bricking yourself alright. I heard it last night. It's a right fucking laugh. It's a fucking classic.'

'But I said that this has gone on far too long,' said Lenny. 'We all have to have our sport, but three days suffering is long enough for anybody. That's what I always say,' said Big Lenny. 'Enough is e-fucking-nough.'

He walked over to me and put his arm around my shoulder and pulled me round into his body. I was still covering myself up and I was slightly off-balance. 'You'll get over it,' he said, and I could feel the laughter ripple through his torso. 'Put it down to experience.'

And he looked at me until I joined him smiling and laughing. You could have heard the bared teeth screams of history's most successful primates up and down the road outside if you had cared to listen. The two of us sat in Edelweiss in the middle of the afternoon convulsed with such intense laughter that it nearly split my sides wide fucking open.

He left soon afterwards and after he had gone and after I had calmed down a bit, I had a thought. And the thought was that Lenny had *chosen* to come and tell me the truth. Of course, I would have changed his manner, but that wasn't that important in the end. He had guided me out of my nightmare, probably at some danger to himself from Adele's boss, a psycho who liked a good prolonged joke involving a lot of suffering in others. And that night I thought to myself that Lenny was like the big brother that I never really had and I admit that in the dark I cried just a little bit at this very moving thought.

# POSTSCRIPT

My professor rang me about a month later. He asked if I was alright. He had seen me around the department and commented that I had been looking a little depressed at times. I made a little joke about body language and depression, pointing out that many people misinterpreted signs of tiredness as signs of actual depression. He said that he didn't normally make that kind of error.

'It's good that you have been working so hard,' said my professor, 'because I have some rather exciting news for you. The defense solicitor liked our work on the analysis of the video-recording of the fatal stabbing, and he has asked us, I mean, me to present our analyses in court. This will be a very public outing for our research. We will probably make the headlines of national newspapers.'

He left a pause for a comment from me, but none came.

'I was just wondering if you could go through the analyses again with me. Just one more time. Let's just call it a little tutorial,' he said. 'I am your eager student here. I must get it all word perfect after all. This is extremely important.'

I said that this was fine.

'Splendid,' he said. He also told me that he had received, several weeks before, the transcripts of the witnesses talking about what had occurred in the drinking club that night. This was the first time that he had mentioned this.

THE BODY'S LITTLE SECRETS

'There is one small thing that might be relevant in those transcripts,' he said. 'Something very small indeed. Do you remember that section of the video in which you can see this little hand gesture occurring before the victim lays his hand on the woman? Do you remember these two fingers coming together then making a very aggressive looking fist?'

'Of course,' I said. 'I remember all that. That was a core part of the analysis.'

'Well, apparently,' said the professor, 'the victim had a long-term relationship with the blonde lady and he's addressing her at that point, according to the witnesses. Let me read what he apparently said to her. "How can you", excuse my language in this next section, "fucking well do this to me? We were so close." And this is the point in time when he apparently makes the gesture. I'm no expert on this, of course, I'm just using my intuition here, but that doesn't affect the interpretation of the gesture in any way, does it?'

He left a gap, a long widening chasm, but I didn't say anything. He had to fill my long, drawn-out silence for me. 'This doesn't significantly affect your expert interpretation, does it?' he asked again. I noticed that he now stressed the word 'expert', passing all responsibility over to me. 'Because the court date has been set and I wouldn't want to look a complete fool in a setting like that. That would be very bad.'

I sat in my office in the dark in front of the bright screen of the video. I could see my own reflection in the monitor. I could see that I looked anxious, very anxious in fact, and I could see that this was not fleeting or squelched. In fact, there was nothing fleeting or squelched about it. I was just relieved that nobody else could see me and my whole facial configuration at that precise instant.

My research had told me all along that iconic gestures and speech work together in a single cognitive representation of the world, but I had set my own views aside to help out my mentor.

To help him out, and I suppose, if I am entirely honest with myself, to prove my own worth. To prove that I was indeed something and not just all talk like the rest of them in this faltering city.

And now it was too late to change my mind. I was committed to a point of view, and so was my professor. I suddenly realized that a fist may at times indicate nothing more than the closing of an iconic gesture representing togetherness. I realized at that precise point that I had been prepared to make convincing sounding arguments on the basis of partial and fragmentary evidence. On the basis of a quick reading of the body language alone, despite all my research to the contrary. I was no better than Cliff. Or Big Lenny. Or any of the rest of them.

I sat there at one end of the telephone and I lied. I said that my interpretation of aggressive intent in the victim still stood and that it could be defended in court under the most stringent cross-examination. 'The most stringent,' I added.

'Splendid,' said my professor. 'Absolutely splendid. I assumed that you would say this. Your research career does depend upon it after all.'

'Oh, and by the way,' added my professor. 'Word of our research appears to be spreading. I have received yet another video-tape to analyze. There was apparently a threat on some doormen by a gang of hooded men armed with baseball bats, which turned very nasty. If you can believe that sort of thing goes on in this city of ours,' he added. 'I personally never witness this sort of thing.'

'Goodness,' I said with all the guile that I could possibly muster in the circumstances.

'Well,' continued my professor. 'This act of threatening behaviour went badly wrong. Very badly wrong. According to the police, it was some dispute about drugs. A new drugs war apparently has broken out in this city. Four men armed with these offensive weapons went to threaten some doormen at a club, but one of the hooded men seemed to get very agitated and started lashing out, before running off. There were some extremely serious injuries incurred as a result. The police this time have asked us to look at the tape to see if our expert analyses can produce any psychological insights into who the attackers might be. They want a psychological profile – some means to identify them.'

I coughed gently down the phone, as if to indicate that this was perhaps, just perhaps, beyond our current competence, a cough to signal that I was about to say something, right there and then, to indicate some reluctance or caution on my part. But the cough stood there for a moment quite alone, embarrassed by its own solitary presence, and then vanished quietly and cowardly into the silence.

'Well, basically,' continued my professor after a pause, 'the police want anything that might be relevant to their enquiries. Do you think that we can help them out here?'

'Of course,' I said. 'We should be able to tell them something. We are the experts after all.' I listened to my own voice saying this and I probably sounded as convincing as I could, under the circumstances. Given how I felt.

My professor's secretary brought me the video-tape to watch the following day. I sat in my room with the light off and the tape on the large screen in front of me. The quality was quite poor on this film. But I recognized the club immediately. I could even make out the steps where the long, snaking queue normally starts.

I played the tape in slow motion and stopped it when the men in the hoods arrived. There was only one close-up in the whole film. A close-up of the largest member of the gang, who had been wielding the baseball bats, in the moments before the violence erupted. He was mouthing something. Something short and to the point.

It was easy to recognize the first word. It has a distinctive shape. It's a bit like watching footballers on the telly. You can always make that word out quite easily. It was the word 'fucking'.

The second word was more difficult. I played it again and again and again until, with familiarity, I could recognize some order in the organization of the mouth. It had a distinctive shape. My heart started to race as it slowly dawned on me what that word might possibly be. I played it again. Then once more. I knew that word alright. I had seen it before. Indeed, I had seen it before from that very same mouth that was now poking through the cloth of that dark hood. It was the word 'tasty'.

I looked at the screen and even through the poor picture quality I was sure that I recognized the size and the shape and the mannerisms of the man who was fleeing. The man whose panic and uncontrollable emotion had evidently started the whole violent conflagration.

It was a man with a very irregular heartbeat rushing down some steps and away from the club, and away from all of this.

*\* END \**

# Author's Note

This book is the story of a psychologist trapped between worlds. It just so happens that I too am a psychologist trapped between worlds, worlds that I sometimes barely understand.

Psychological science now tells us that the thinking underlying speaking relates most closely to the hand movements and gestures that we make when speaking. The hands unconsciously draw images to accompany talk, without the benefit of a mental lexicon, but still perfectly meaningful. There is unconscious meaning in the hands, spontaneously created and unconsciously expressed, as one psychologist put it. Indeed, the hand movements that accompany speech are now recognised as parts of the same basic underlying process of thought in action.

Thinking impacts on other nonverbal behaviour as well: head movements, head nods and shakes, eye contact, gaze direction, sniffs, yawns, lip licks, posture changes, fidgets, self-adaptors, foot slides, foot kicks, foot taps, and the list goes on. It was once said by a famous psychologist that 'you cannot not communicate'. Even silence and stillness communicate; indeed, they communicate a great deal. We have dozens of words for silence. In the book the Lenny character called it 'a stand off', 'a glare', 'being fucking difficult'; he liked to talk, no, he had to talk. We use communication for our own ends.

The story of Matt is ultimately about the way that we fool others and the way that we can fool ourselves.

Nonverbal communication is what the narrator of the novel studies for a living. It happens to be very similar to my own academic interests.

Obviously Matt's story is a work of fiction, but it is no accident that I had my narrator moving north from Cambridge. At about this time, I graduated with a PhD. from the University of Cambridge and moved north to Sheffield to my first academic post. It is an uncomfortable narrative for many reasons. It is about my younger self, and it is often disquieting to look back. Life, after all, is full of regrets. It is now something of a cultural cliché, to ask what advice you would give to your younger self. But these were difficult times, indeed difficult and tumultuous times, and in retrospect I can see what some of my (or his) problems were.

It all happened in the context of Margaret Thatcher. She famously said: 'I think we have gone through a period when too many children and people have been given to understand "I have a problem, it is the Government's job to cope with it!" or "I have a problem, I will go and get a grant to cope with it!" "I am homeless, the Government must house me!" and so they are casting their problems on society and who is society? There is no such thing! There are individual men and women and there are families'. It was all now to be just about the individual, and the survival of the fittest individual.

When I watched Margaret Thatcher in an interview in 1979 my life changed. My attention was not drawn to her threats and promises, or her arguments. I was interested in her nonverbal communication, her gestures, her hesitations, the basic structure of the interview, the turn-taking, the interruptions, the overlapping talk of interviewer and interviewee lasting five seconds (which sounded like an eternity), and where this all came from.

When I listened to the tape of the interview carefully, I

thought that I heard something in her speech and I noticed something in her body language. I thought that she might be subconsciously cueing in her interviewer with a series of 'turn-yielding signals'. More specifically, she cued them in with a rapid fall in pitch at the end of a clause. She didn't let her pitch drop too low (a trough of 167 Hz compared with 141 Hz for genuine turn-final utterances), but what she did do was let her pitch drop very quickly on these turn-disputed utterances (a span of 463 milliseconds for this drop). She also sometimes terminated an iconic gesture.

However, she rarely used 'filled' pauses, like 'ums' or 'ahs' — she only used four in the whole interview. Filled pauses are effective floor holding devices – they protect the floor for about 600 milliseconds afterwards. Instead she made time for cognitive planning by extending the length of certain syllables or drawling. Drawl is another turn-yielding cue, and the more turn-yielding cues displayed by a speaker, the higher the probability of the listener (or in this case, the interviewer) trying to take the floor.

I, therefore, had evidence which seemed to suggest that her idiosyncratic interview behaviour depended upon interviewer-initiated interruption which she then contested (leaving the interviewer a little puzzled). The locations of these interviewer-initiated interruptions could be mathematically predicted on the basis of cues in her own speech.

In other words, the high proportion of overlapping speech (academic jargon for interrupting one another) was not simply a case of her underlying personality coming through, rather this joint-behaviour was a product of a more complex situation (although her underlying personality might well have had a role in how the breakdown in turn-taking was finally resolved). My guess was that her speech training from a voice coach at the Royal National Theatre in the years previous to this, which had successfully lowered the pitch of her voice and apparently encouraged her to drawl rather than use filled pauses to make more time for cognitive planning, was largely responsible.

This was how I saw social behaviour from then on. This was my discourse. But I was also a witness to the 'de-industrialisation' of the North, the political denial of 'society' as a possible force for good, or even as a useful concept, and existential crises of one sort or another all around me. I became interested in people, their lives and their experiences, which might be an odd confession for someone with a PhD. in psychology from Cambridge, but psychology can be a reductionist science, where the person is somehow lost. If truth be told, I was shocked by what I saw when I arrived in Sheffield. I lived up in Crookes with an unemployed steelworker two doors down and another opposite, and more toward the bottom of the street and many towards the top, as the houses start to overlook the Bole Hills. I started to write about what I was witnessing in my street and the next street and then further afield for the *Guardian* Grassroots page, edited by the late John Course, and for *New Society* edited by Paul Barker.

The novel, then, is about my coming of age (and the narrator's, of course) and the hard lessons that I (and he) had to learn. I published my detailed micro-analyses of Margaret Thatcher's interviews and associated turn-taking problems and attracted some very positive publicity in the media and elsewhere. The 'Iron Lady', I argued, was born in these micro-interview battles. That, at least, was my thesis, and I was applauded for it.

And then the real dilemma opened up in front of me (my narrator has a similar problem). Was I now an expert on power and dominance in all interactions, was I now an expert on all nonverbal communication, wherever it took place, whoever it involved? After all, it is one thing talking to fellow academics, it is quite another to attempt to explain my thesis to the unemployed steelworkers and miners, now living in her individualistic and self-reliant 'non-society'. What truths did they hear? What did I actually know about life out there on the streets?

But one thing did become clear - we all have to leave our own little cave one day and survive with the little that we do know.

For me (and for my narrator) it was a process of major discovery with many shocks along the way, as I set out quite alone to apply my newly acquired knowledge of nonverbal communication to other people's lives, where the unemployed steelworkers and miners were fighting the government. 'No society', like silence, can mean many things.

Now that is a semiotic conundrum of the highest order, even I could recognise this, and I suppose, therefore, it was some sort of start for both me and my narrator on our professional and personal journey in this strange and unfamiliar land. Even though there was no society, all of us were trying to improve our position in our own way – including Margaret Thatcher trying to dominate her interviewers.

And then there was my older brother whom I worshipped. His death during my first year in Sheffield was the hardest part of it all.

# Acknowledgements

Andrew Motion published my first collection of observations in '*Survivors of Steel City*', published by Chatto & Windus in 1986. I went on to write '*Making It: The Reality of Today's Entrepreneurs*' (Weidenfeld & Nicolson), '*On the Ropes: Boxing as a Way of Life*' (Victor Gollancz) and '*The Shadows of Boxing*' (Orion). The books got darker as the times got more desperate and I draw upon some of these observations extensively in the present work of fiction. 'The Shadows of Boxing', as much about the shadows in society as about boxing itself, provides the base for this novel, and I thank Orion for allowing me to do this. These essentially ethnographic earlier works were all published some time ago, and they read now like historical works about the changing of an industrial society, which I suppose they are. The new book hopefully brings those times to life, and puts the protagonist, who like me happens to be a psychologist fresh from Cambridge, and his discomforts (and it has to be said psychology itself) clearly in the frame. My agent, Robert Kirby from United Agents, has never been anything but incredibly supportive, and we have been together for a very long time, and I offer him my wholehearted thanks for recognising something in my somewhat diverse work from the start, including the present novel. The enthusiasm of my publisher Martin Rynja was an absolute joy from the start.